THE UGLY GODDESS

THE UGLY GODDESS

ELSA MARSTON

Cricket Books

Chicago

Library of Congress Cataloging-in-Publication Data

Marston, Elsa.
  The ugly goddess / Elsa Marston.-- 1st ed.
    p. cm.
Summary: Fourteen-year-old Princess Meret is unhappy with her future as
consort of the Egyptian god Amun, especially after meeting Hector, a
handsome Greek soldier, but when she is kidnapped, it is up to Hector
and a young servant boy to help rescue her with the aid of the goddess
Taweret.
  ISBN 0-8126-2667-2 (cloth : alk. paper)
  1. Egypt—History—To 332 B.C.—Juvenile fiction.
  [1. Egypt—History—To 332 B.C.—Fiction.] I. Title.
  PZ7.M356755 Ug 2002
  [Fic]—dc21

                                                      2002004674

FMA

FOR THOSE WHO HAD FAITH IN THE
GODDESS . . .

MY FAMILY—ILIYA, RAMSAY, AMAHL,
AND RAIF—AND MY FRIENDS IN THE
BLOOMINGTON CHILDREN'S AUTHORS:
ELAINE, KEIKO, JOY, MARCIA, MARILYN,
PAM, AND PAT.

ANCIENT EGYPT ON THE EVE OF CHANGE . . .
THE TIME IS 525 B.C.

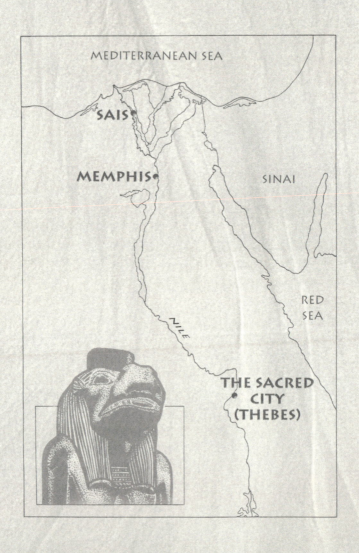

MEDITERRANEAN SEA

SAIS•

MEMPHIS•

SINAI

NILE

RED SEA

THE SACRED CITY (THEBES)

CHAPTER 1

Bata paused in his sweeping as he watched Smendes at work. The master was almost finished with the statue and had already started polishing the fine greenish black stone. In places it gleamed as though filled with divine life . . . yet details of the feet and tail were still only roughed in.

Surely, thought Bata, that statue must be the master's finest work. Surely it would be the most beautiful creation in all his long years as Egypt's greatest sculptor.

Gazing at such perfection, the boy couldn't help wishing, as he had many times before, that the gods had bestowed some sort of gift on *him*, too. But they hadn't. And why should they bother with him, anyway? His lot in this world was to sweep up stone chips, run errands, and hoist heavy loads in his strong arms.

Seeing Bata idle, Smendes rested his chisel, straightened up, and frowned. "What are you doing, boy? I don't see the floor clean yet. I told you, someone from the palace is coming this afternoon to check on the royal order. Get on with your work, and be quick about it."

1

As Bata hastily started pushing the broom around again, Smendes sank down on a three-legged stool, his face twisted in pain. Bata hated to see the old man like that. If only he could do something to ease the master's misery! But there was only one thing—and Smendes soon thought of it.

"No, boy, put down your broom and go get me some beer, there's a good lad."

Bata promptly ran out of the workshop into the bright sunshine of midday. The weather was fairly warm for late winter, but he was glad to have his short jacket on. He headed for a tavern a few streets away, where the owner poured out her brew with a generous hand and the beer was always fresh, cool, and as clean as any.

With a jug full of frothy liquid in each hand, Bata hurried back through the narrow alleys, trying not to stumble and slosh the beer. It wasn't easy, not with his long clumsy legs and feet. That's what came of shooting up so fast. At fifteen he was already taller than most men—and having done hard work all his life, strong. But clumsy. No, how could he ever do anything fine, if he couldn't even carry a jug of beer without spilling it?

As he shuffled down a dusty passageway, Bata thought about his master. The sickness in the master's teeth made the old man crazy sometimes. But his heart, Bata feared, must be the real trouble. A *good* heart—the gods knew that for certain—but so tired now. Even though the beer seemed to quiet the teeth, maybe it was too strong for the heart.

Preoccupied with his thoughts, Bata nearly stumbled. Taking greater care, he hustled along—until he turned the corner near Smendes' workshop. There he stopped short. The alley was choked by a noisy crowd. A fight, maybe? Getting a firmer grip on his two jugs, Bata prepared to edge through. Soon, though, he found his way blocked and craned his neck to see what was going on.

A young Greek in a military tunic seemed to be at the center of the trouble. He looked rattled and angry; the crowd had him backed up to the mud-brick wall, hemming him in but keeping a distance.

As Bata picked up some of the shouts, he began to understand. The Greek, arrogant fool, had thought he could just help himself to a handful of the fruit seller's figs and walk off. But the old woman had yelled, and within seconds every idler in the neighborhood had come running.

A whole platoon of Greek soldiers, to be sure, could more or less do as they pleased. But *one* fellow, and a young one, was quite another matter. Here was one Greek intruder who wouldn't try pushing Egyptians around again!

A pebble flew, hitting the wall behind the young soldier. Then a pomegranate caught him on the shoulder, dribbling down his tunic, and an egg mashed against his cheek. He shouted in anger but had no weapon, and the crowd only jeered. A stone hit him, and a fish. As he tried to break out of the advancing semicircle, the missiles came faster.

Bata watched, fascinated. The Greek was getting what he deserved. No doubt he'd gone swaggering through the streets of Egypt's capital city as if he owned the place. And then, adding injury to insult, he'd tried to steal from an honest, hardworking Egyptian. This would teach him a lesson.

But the next moment, Bata caught his breath. A sharp stone had hit the Greek squarely on the temple, making him stagger and nearly fall. The lesson was getting out of hand. If the mob tasted blood, Bata thought, they might even kill the Greek. That would mean major trouble. The foreign garrison would retaliate, and Pharaoh's own military officers would have to back them up.

Besides, it wasn't right—some twenty people against one young man. It was too much, no matter how insolent the victim had been at the start.

Without further thought, Bata set down the two jugs of beer and waded into the crowd, elbowing people aside. When he reached the Greek, he grabbed him by the arm and, using his own body as a shield, pulled him through the semicircle of attackers. A moment later, the protests burst forth.

"Hey, Bata, what d'you think you're doing?"

"Let us deal with that Greek—he's a thief!"

Bata ignored the heckling as he pushed the Greek ahead of him down the alley. At first the young man did not resist, but soon he started to struggle, twisting around to get a look at his unknown rescuer.

"Hurry," mumbled Bata, still hardly aware of what he was doing. "My shop's ahead—you'll be safe there." He gave the Greek a good prod in the ribs, and they both began to run. Just in time. The crowd, recovering from their surprise, had started to follow.

As Bata shoved the bewildered Greek through the narrow door of the shop, the men inside stopped their work to stare. Smendes, still slumped on the stool, pulled himself up with effort and stood. He was the master here.

"What is this?" he demanded in his thin voice. "Bata, what's all that shouting? And who is this person?"

The Greek, now that he appeared to be safe, quickly regained command of himself. Like Smendes, who was standing as straight as he could, the young man drew himself up—as though to look down on all Egyptians once more. He was almost the same height as Bata but maybe a couple of years older, to judge from the soft beard on his chin.

Just then Bata remembered the two jugs of beer he'd set against a wall. Gone for good by now. That would mean some harsh words and another swat. Of course, it would be mostly the pain in Smendes that snarled—but Bata knew he'd earned his punishment. What business was it of his, after all, rescuing this Greek fool?

The Greek fool interrupted his worries. "Your boy doesn't know me," he said, addressing Smendes in lofty tones, although not without a slight quaver in his voice. "And obviously neither do you, old man. I am Hector, son of Leander."

Leander! That name did mean something. The startled look on Smendes' face and the surprised murmurs from the other workers proved it. Leander was commander in chief of all the Greek mercenary forces stationed in Egypt's capital city, Saïs. Everyone knew how much Pharaoh relied on this Greek army, and how above all the other officers he favored Leander, a skillful, battle-hardened leader who controlled his men with a firm but fair hand, according to the common talk.

Hector spoke again in the ringing silence that had suddenly filled the workshop. "Your boy did me a good turn. He seems a different sort from the rest of the rabble in your streets."

At that, Bata glanced out the door. The rabble had totally disappeared, and Bata saw why: two Greek soldiers had just come striding down the alley, tall men in full military uniform. They stopped by the entrance to the workshop, their forms filling the doorway, and Bata saw the alarm in Smendes' face.

Turning to leave with the two soldiers, Hector paused and looked at Bata. "It will not be forgotten," he said. Then the three Greeks were gone.

Bata was left to face his master, beerless. But another thought had just occurred to him: that Hector, son of Leander—he spoke the Egyptian language! Not as it should be spoken, of course. After all, he was just a foreigner. But how did he know it at all, when most other Greeks couldn't say even two words?

CHAPTER 2

In a light, airy room in the palace, Princess Meret sat on a delicately carved wooden stool to have her hair trimmed. With an abrupt wriggle, she shifted her weight, then twitched her shoulders and hitched around again.

"Sit still," commanded Tiaa the nurse. She had no hesitation in speaking sharply to a princess. After all, she had been the palace nurse since long before Meret's baby years. "Now let that poor woman finish working on your hair. You'll drive her crazy with your antics."

Meret glared at her old nurse. "I can't help it! I wish I could smash things—I wish I could throw myself out the window! But here I have to sit, perfectly still like a statue."

"Yes, indeed you do." Tiaa folded her thin arms in a gesture meant to put an end to all discussion. "Make up your mind right now—you will have to submit to what is required of you."

What was required at the moment was nothing much: simply to let Aset cut her hair off, a routine that Meret went through every few weeks so that her wig would fit smoothly.

As her last days in the palace grew near, however, she felt like rebelling against absolutely everything.

"I have *nice* hair," she moaned. "You used to tell me, Tiaa, how my father would hold me and run his fingers through my baby curls and laugh. And now it has to be cut off forever, just so I can wear a huge, heavy, ugly wig for the rest of my life."

"Hush, child," said Tiaa, irritated. "You are a princess, the daughter of Pharaoh, and, above all, the future wife of the god. You must look the part at all times—a fine wig is essential." For just an instant she paused. "And no one, except the few servants closest to you, will ever again see those curls of yours."

As Tiaa finished her speech, Meret thought her voice sounded a tiny bit choked. She looked up at the nurse in surprise. Was there actually a tear in Tiaa's eye? No, impossible to say for sure, because Tiaa had quickly turned away to inspect the fine linen sheath that was waiting to be slipped over the girl's head. The moment passed, and Meret's passion returned.

"I never wanted to be the Divine Wife! I don't see why it has to be forced on me. I'll run away, I'll kill myself, I'll—"

"Hush!" Now Tiaa was truly shocked. "If anyone heard you say such things, it would—"

"Would what?" Meret countered. "Make them understand?"

"In any case, it would change nothing, my child. You know that as well as I do."

Tiaa turned to glare at Aset and the other two servants in the room. Meekly they lowered their gazes. The command of silence regarding anything that went on in the royal chambers was well observed.

Meret slumped on her hairdressing stool. Here she was, fourteen years old, almost a woman. Yet she felt as helpless as an infant. She knew very well that she was behaving badly, childishly, unworthily — but she couldn't stop herself. "If I'd known this would happen to me," she fretted, "I'd have made sure to have an older sister and I'd have made *her* be the Divine Wife. After all, I am the first princess, and my wishes must be granted."

Looking up at Tiaa in defiance, Meret caught the glimmer of a smile on the old woman's face, which only upset her all the more. "Anyway," she continued, "why do I have to go *now*? The Divine Wife is just going to adopt me as her successor — I won't even get to *be* the god's wife as long as she is alive. Why can't the whole thing wait until — until later, sometime, so I can stay here?"

"This is the proper time," said Tiaa officiously. "Now stop your arguing. You have known for years that you would be the next Divine Wife, and you never resented it before."

"How do you know how I felt? Anyway, when I was younger, it all seemed so far off. And I didn't know any better. Now I do. I can read and think and — "

At this, the nurse threw up her hands. "There we have it! I knew it was unwise of your father — may the gods protect him — to allow you to learn the art of writing. It's not right for a woman to do the work of scribes and priests. But with no son to train, he would do it — he would go ahead and have you taught. I remember him saying — the gods bless him — your mind was as quick as any boy's. The very idea."

"Yes, it is — and I'm glad he did!" said Meret fiercely. "I know more about the world than you think, Tiaa, and I want to go on learning — and not only from texts. I do not want to be imprisoned in a temple for all my days, stuck with those tiresome old ceremonies and rituals."

As she caught her breath after this speech, her words — *I know more about the world* — echoed in Meret's mind. She had said them to someone else recently . . . who could it have been? Yes, that Greek. That curiously bold young Greek. Now, in the same way that he had intruded, the memories insisted on returning.

The first time, he had come with two or three important Greek officers for a conference with Pharaoh in the council chambers. Meret, who had been talking with her father and was about to leave, had lingered for a few minutes. The Greeks could be counted on to provide some amusement, with their brash, bumptious ways. The young man had been supposed to act as an interpreter, but it seemed he was not paying close attention. Several times one or another of the officers had had to call him by name. Although Meret had glanced at him only occasionally, she was aware of his almost constant gaze upon her. She had thought it most improper. But . . . interesting.

A few days later, they had actually spoken. This time they'd met by chance in a corridor, as Meret returned from a garden with one of her servants. He'd mumbled something about being in the palace on business and getting lost in the many halls; but when she had offered a servant to show him the way out, he had simply smiled, bowed, and introduced himself. Hector was his name.

"It appears, most gracious Princess," he'd said with an amused look in his eye, "that you attend important meetings on military matters. Does that sort of thing interest you?"

She'd bristled and replied without hesitation. "Certainly it does. And Pharaoh values my presence. I know more about the world than you might think."

"Very good." His smile had grown broader, but Meret detected a trace of embarrassment in it. He then turned his attention to the well-worn papyrus manuscript in her hands.

"It's about medicine," she'd told him loftily, "the treatment of pain and disease. Actually, it's an ancient text, but the doctors still find it useful today."

"Medicine? You study medical matters as well?"

"And why not?"

"But . . . women aren't supposed to know such things."

"Women help their sisters to bring babies into the world—why shouldn't they know about other things that happen to the human body? Your views seem to be very old-fashioned, I must say."

With a laugh the Greek had conceded the point, but not for long. "Now, you don't mean to tell me you are actually reading those strange marks that you Egyptians use, all those pretty little pictures. Surely *that* is not something for women's minds."

"Ah!" she'd answered proudly. "I admit that not many women learn to read and write, because it is indeed extremely difficult. But I have worked hard and have learned, which proves that my mind is as good as any man's. Look." Unrolling the papyrus a little, she showed him a passage about the circulation of blood, read it—with a few errors, but how would he know?—and looked up at him in triumph. As he moved closer to her, following her finger on the text, she noticed a pleasing fragrance, good leather and sandalwood.

Then her servant had coughed quietly, and Meret knew that she must move on. It certainly wouldn't do for Tiaa or any of the less amiable servants to find her talking with a Greek in such a casual fashion.

For a moment Meret's memories touched her with a pleasant warmth, but she pushed them away as Tiaa's voice broke in. Motioning for Aset to step aside, the nurse came and stood close to Meret.

"Dear child," she said gently, her gnarled brown hand resting on the wide collar that protected Meret's shoulders from the prickly clippings, "I know this is hard for you. But you must look at it differently. Think of the honor—Divine

Wife, consort of the great god Amun! The highest honor for a woman in all of Egypt—no, in all the world! Such an honor befalls a daughter of Pharaoh only once in fifty years or so. Think of the riches, the power that will be in your hands—"

"Riches?" Meret sat up straight. "I have all I need. And just what is that wonderful power in the Divine Wife's hands? Nothing! The priests have all the real power—you know that as well as I do. I won't be allowed to do anything on my own. I'll be pampered and coddled and become a lazy little nothing. I don't want to turn into a—a cabbage, Tiaa. All I want is to live my life as I wish."

With a snort of impatience, Tiaa went on more forcefully. "Then think, my dear princess, of what this means for Egypt. Think of the long years when Egypt's glory languished, and how Egypt is now again supreme among all nations. Think—"

"Yes, yes, I know all that. I've heard it all my life," said Meret with a weary sigh. "Egypt is mighty. Egypt can vanquish any foe. And of course it's because the great Amun is happily married that Egypt is strong."

"Take care, Princess—you speak too lightly!"

Meret twitched. Some of the shorn hairs had worked their way under her protective collar, making her even more irritable. "I understand about duty, Tiaa. I have heard everything you can say to me. But when I think of how *alone* I will be in the Sacred City, how far from everyone I know, from everyone who means anything to me . . ." She looked up at her nurse, and her eyes began to fill. "I'd thought that you, at least, would be allowed to live there with me. But now I'm told that no one from the palace can stay, that I will see no one but the priests and attendants of the Divine Wife— *ever!* Tiaa, it scares me . . ." Now there was no stopping the tears.

With a hand under Meret's chin, Tiaa gently lifted the girl's face. "You will not be alone," she said softly. "The goddess will be with you. That's why your father—the gods bless him—had the statue made for you. You know that a statue of the Great One, Taweret herself, has never before been made especially for a princess. This is yet another high honor bestowed on you."

"Yes, Taweret will be with me." As Tiaa released her, Meret's tears subsided. Almost immediately, however, she looked up with another challenge. "Tiaa, *why* Taweret? Why didn't my father choose another deity, Hathor, for instance, or Isis? Surely that would have been more appropriate, wouldn't it? I've never known quite what to think of Taweret. She's so—so . . ." Meret gave an odd little twitch of the shoulders, as though shrugging off something that made her uncomfortable.

"Mind your words, Princess, when speaking of the deities," said Tiaa sharply. "Taweret is the great protector, and it is appropriate for her to accompany you."

"Will I be in need of protection in the Sacred City? Is that what you're telling me?"

"Now, now," Tiaa replied, with more restraint than Meret had expected. "We all benefit from the protection of Taweret, every one of us. Indeed, her main concern is with women and children—"

"But especially at childbirth," Meret argued, her voice taking on a sarcastic edge. "Very appropriate, indeed. And how many children will the great Amun give me?"

Tiaa answered with exaggerated patience. "My dear princess. The great Amun will not give you actual children, to bear in pain and—and messiness, as is the lot of ordinary women. But you will be his wife and"—she paused as though thinking of the best way to put it—"your ceremonial role will stimulate him in such a way as to make all of Egypt fertile and productive. That's why, dear Meret, it is most essential that the goddess Taweret be your special protector, you above all."

Slumping once more, Meret turned aside. *This gets very difficult to understand,* she said to herself. *Am I really supposed to believe it?* Aloud she said to Tiaa, "Very well, that may be as you say. Taweret is the Great One, a blessed and benevolent goddess, and I'm glad she'll be watching over me — for whatever reason. I just wish that the beautiful statue my father ordered for me might have been a bit more . . . beautiful."

Tiaa opened her mouth to object, but Aset was quicker. Putting down her sharp hair-trimming knife, the hairdresser spoke as though she must say something or burst. "O Princess, all the royal city is talking about that statue! The Supervisor of Weavers told me, and the Keeper of Keys told him, and the Provisioner of Royal Gifts — who goes to the sculptor's workshop himself — told *him,* so it is certainly true. Everyone says that no statue of such perfection has ever been made, not even in the old times. They say that the goddess herself is guiding the hand of the sculptor. Surely this is a good omen, O Princess."

"Enough, Aset," said the nurse dryly. "It's time to bring this discussion to a close. I must attend to a thousand other things necessary for your departure, Princess." Taking the other servants with her, Tiaa left the room.

Aset finished the shearing of Meret's soft black hair. Instead of sweeping up the cropped curls, however, she again made an unexpected move.

Kneeling before Meret, her head low, she said, "O Princess, forgive me — it is not my place to speak of this. I know that everything the respected Tiaa has said is true, and I rejoice in your honor. But . . . just the same, my heart must speak the truth, too. O Princess, I . . ."

"What is it?" Although surprised, Meret was not annoyed at Aset's speech. She had always liked the woman, a quiet person with a plain, kind face. Sometimes just her gentle presence gave Meret the sense of being mothered, even though the servant was barely ten years older than the princess.

"I—I hardly dare . . ."

"Speak, Aset," said Meret. "And then get on with your work."

"I mourn, O Princess, because . . . you will never have a husband."

Meret drew back, amazed at her servant's boldness. Then she laughed with bitter humor. "Oh? Isn't the god himself husband enough?"

Aset glanced around, then went on in hushed tones. "The god himself, or his statue of solid gold, is not the same as a real man of bones and flesh. I wish for another life for you, my princess. I wish you could have a real husband to walk with and laugh with and—and argue with, and one day go together with to your eternal life in the West. I wish for babies for you, a little boy to hold in your arms and guide as he grows, and a little girl to play with. I wish, my princess, that the life *every* woman wants could be—"

"Aset, enough! You should not say such things."

Immediately the woman broke off her surprising speech. She went about her work in silence, then bowed and hurried from the room.

Left alone, Meret felt not only astonishment but uneasiness at the servant's words. What did the woman mean, speaking in such a manner to her princess—almost as if casting a spell! Did she really think that anything could be changed? Yet Meret was touched, both by Aset's love for her and by what the woman had said. For a moment she wondered what it would be like to look forward to the love of a husband and children, like every other girl in Egypt. Her own mother, she'd always been told, had been a happy woman, cherished by an adoring husband. Meret often wished she could remember better.

Anyway, it made no sense to talk of marriage now, and Aset should not have spoken as she did.

Two servants entered, carrying a tray laden with tiny glass bottles and gold-trimmed alabaster jars. Meret sat quietly while they spread the precious green powder on her eyelids. Next they drew careful black borders on the rims of her eyes and applied the black paint more lavishly on her eyebrows, extending the graceful curves almost to her hairline. Meret endured it in silence, exhausted by her unhappiness, her futile arguments with Tiaa, and then that disturbing speech by Aset. But her mind was busy.

Here I sit, as I will have to sit every morning for the rest of my life, being fussed over . . . a pampered little doll, unable to do anything for myself. I wonder what would happen if I ever had to face real hardship. What if I were dumped in the desert? Could I even survive?

When she was dressed and her face properly painted, the princess left her chambers and headed for one of the gardens scattered throughout the palace grounds. Maybe a little time by the pool, breathing soft air scented by rare trees and flowers, would calm and refresh her. Still, she couldn't escape her troubled thoughts.

Everyone wants me to be something different from what I am. All I want is my freedom . . . to learn, and think, and enjoy my life as I wish. And someday have enough knowledge to help my father guide Egypt. But how can I do anything, imprisoned in a temple? Is there any way of escape?

CHAPTER 3

Two days passed after Bata went out to bring back beer and instead brought back a Greek. The atmosphere in Smendes' workshop, Bata felt, was changing. The other workers now looked at him in a different way and were quick to ridicule and criticize.

Once, nervously clumsy, Bata dropped a block of fine alabaster, cracking off one large corner. "Fool, misfit!" the shop manager growled. "You should work in a pigsty — though you'd probably break even the pigs." The other men's tentative snickers grew to guffaws, until the master's high voice rose above them and immediately commanded silence.

"Look to yourselves!" Smendes said. "There's no man here who has never slipped. The boy does his best — no one can deny that." Smendes turned back to his work, but continued to scold. "And don't look down on him. The ability to carve stone is not the only gift worth having. Who knows what form the divine may take in this boy?"

The men were quiet, and the moment passed. But Bata knew their eyes were hard.

Although the master had defended him, the boy noted that since he had returned with the Greek, even Smendes now rarely slipped in a kind word among his scolding ones. Finally, finding the old man at rest for a moment and apparently not in much pain, Bata asked him, "What is it, Master? Everyone seems angry with me."

Smendes turned his faded eyes toward Bata and sighed. "The men are uneasy because of the Greeks, boy."

"Yes, but what—" Bata was embarrassed and confused. He knew that the Greek troops were resented, even though Pharaoh thought they would be needed in case of war. Rumors constantly raced through the marketplace. Many people worried that the Persians, having so easily taken over the lands to the east, would soon be eyeing Egypt. Everyone had an opinion, loud and vigorous; no one, of course, had answers.

Now the old man's cracked voice grew stronger. "Why, you brought Greeks here, boy, under our very roof! What if they decide to come back? Do you want your master's workshop to be known all over the city as a refuge for any Greek fool who gets himself into trouble? That would look disloyal."

Bata hung his head. He had not thought of that. But at the same time, it all seemed so wrong to him—making such a big thing of such a small act. He had simply wanted to help someone who faced unfair odds. Where was the disloyalty in that?

Smendes turned away and resumed his work on the statue. Plainly, he wanted nothing more to do with Bata for now. Nor was there time for talk. Word had come from the palace to hurry with the order, and all the men were working hard. Several pieces were ready for delivery. There were exquisite bowls and vases carved of stone ranging from translucent alabaster to the hardest basalt, and, most spectacular, two granite sphinxes in Pharaoh's likeness, each the size of a real lion.

The crowning piece, however, was the statue of the goddess Taweret. As everyone in Saïs knew, it was Pharaoh's personal gift to the princess, made expressly to accompany her to the Sacred City.

Carved from dense and flawless stone, the statue stood about as high as a large goose. The body, upright on two sturdy legs like those of a lion, was that of a pregnant hippopotamus with human breasts. The head resembled both a crocodile and a hippopotamus, and the tip of a tongue protruded from huge, toothy jaws. The goddess's arms, human in form, ended in feline paws, and her cowlike ears were similar to those of Hathor, the cow-headed goddess of love and marriage.

Smendes was now laboring over the thick crocodile-like tail that extended downward from Taweret's shoulders and was still attached too solidly to the lower part of her back. Carving the smallest detail to perfection, the master sculptor was taking his time and would not be rushed.

Surely the goddess was within that stone, Bata thought. All the deities must be pleased with Smendes' work. But the hours were numbered. What would happen if the master could not finish the statue in time?

The old man proved to be right about the Greeks. They did come back, that very afternoon. Once again the narrow doorway to the workshop darkened, and the son of Leander stood there with two soldiers.

"Good afternoon," he said, before Smendes could offer a welcome that everyone knew would be false. "As I told you, Hector, the son of Leander, does not forget a favor. Where is the boy?"

With a short gesture Smendes indicated Bata, who felt compelled to step forward and make an awkward little bow. "I did nothing," he mumbled in embarrassment.

"Nonetheless," said Hector, "I wish you to have something, to remind you of the honor of the Greeks." As he took a small leather purse from his waist, one of the soldiers approached Bata and held out a garment of finely woven black wool.

Bata instinctively backed away. He knew he should not receive such gifts. He wished he were somewhere else altogether. But Smendes had turned aside, leaving Bata on his own. Afraid to refuse, Bata had to accept.

"I—I thank you," he murmured, feeling dark looks directed toward his back from every corner of the workshop. He glanced ruefully at the objects in his hands, then placed them in a corner near the master's workbench. The cloak would come in handy . . . but that purse, full of the foreigners' coins? Bata had no idea how to use the small pieces of metal; few Egyptians did.

"Very well!" Now Hector's voice took on a different tone, as if he were glad to have that job done. But he did not turn to leave. Instead, his gaze started to wander around the cluttered room, and a more relaxed, open expression came over his face.

"I've never visited an Egyptian workshop," he said. "I'd like to look around."

This brought back Smendes' full attention—he could hardly ignore such an open demand. "You may do so," he said shortly. "But I must get on with my work. Bata, you can answer any questions our visitor may have."

A double punishment, Bata realized. He would have to manage a difficult encounter the best he could, while the son of Leander would have to accept the attention of the lowliest worker in the shop. Anyway, it couldn't last very long. After a few minutes of Bata's clumsy, shy speech, surely the Greek would be glad to leave.

Hector dismissed the two soldiers, who looked relieved and hustled out to the alley. As all the men in the shop got back to work, Bata led the visitor around the noisy, cramped room. Hector seemed genuinely interested and impressed by the graceful shapes and thin sides of the stone vessels.

Bata's spirits started to lift. His master's workshop was the most renowned in the city, probably in all of Egypt. Even though he did only the most humble tasks, he could take pride in being part of that workshop.

"We do fine work in Egypt, the best in the world," Bata went on, stammering less now. "For a long time, my master says, it wasn't so. The country was ruled by ignorant foreigners. But ever since the days of the great King Psamtik, my master says, the country has been strong again. We try to do work as fine as they did long ago, when Egypt's kings built the Great Pyramids."

At that point Bata caught himself. Why was he talking like this? He'd had so few chances in his life to speak with pride, and now he'd just been babbling, even when the Greek's gaze started to wander.

At Bata's last words, however, Hector turned back with interest. "The Great Pyramids—I've seen them! And the Sphinx rising from the sands. Amazing! That's the good thing about being stationed in Egypt—there are so many marvels to see."

For a moment Hector appeared in Bata's eyes not as a Greek, but as an ordinary person who could be impressed by Egypt's wonders. It made Bata stand straighter. And that, he discovered, allowed him actually to look down on the Greek, by a few fingers' width.

Encouraged, he tried to say more. "All these things are for the palace, for a great occasion."

"Yes," said Hector, "I know something important is going on. In fact, I know more about Egypt than you might think. As you see, I know your language."

"You speak well," said Bata, and had an immediate misgiving. Would that comment be called disloyal to Egypt?

Hector leapt into the opening. "The study of languages is my gift. I learned the language of the Phoenicians while we were stationed in Sidon, and I am making excellent progress in the Egyptian language, difficult as it is. Already my father depends on my services. I often go to meetings between our officers and your king and his generals."

So that explained his ability to speak Egyptian. Bata, who could not even imagine learning another people's tongue, was impressed.

By now they had completed the tour of the workshop. Bata hoped the visitor would be on his way, but Hector showed no signs of it. Pausing at the bench where Smendes was working, he gazed at the statue for such a long time that Bata was afraid the old man would make some peevish remark.

"That is very fine work," said Hector at last. "I have never seen better."

Bata caught the grimace of annoyance on Smendes' face: who did this fool think he was, bestowing praise on the master sculptor! But Hector did not seem to have noticed. He thanked Smendes and turned toward the door. Bata, thinking it the proper thing to do, went with him a few steps into the alley. He was astonished to hear the Greek's next words.

"I want to talk with you some more. I want to understand some things better about the Egyptians. And it's useful for me to—to get accustomed to different ways of speaking, you see. Different dialects and accents. Different classes. When you're through work, meet me at the tavern they call Ipu's, on the other side of the canal. I'll be there at sundown."

Bata stared, open-mouthed. What could a highborn Greek possibly want with an ignorant nobody like Bata, a poor boy with little more to his name than the dirty cloth around his hips? Were the Greek's words an *order*—and if so, what if Bata refused? If his fellow workers learned he had arranged to meet the foreigner again, it would look bad, indeed. He was struck dumb with indecision.

Then, as the sun sent slanting rays down the alley, a beam of light fell on the Greek, bringing golden highlights to his curly brown hair. He squinted, and once more Bata had the sense that the young man standing before him was not a hostile foreigner, but simply a person, like himself. He could see clearly the welt on the Greek's forehead where the stone had struck on that fateful afternoon . . . a stone that seemed to have marked Bata in some way as well. Bata felt something mysterious in his heart overpower his judgment.

"All right," he said. "If I can help you learn more about Egypt, I will try."

CHAPTER 4

In the palace stables a handsome young mare was foaling, and Princess Meret wanted to watch. The start of new life, she reasoned, was one of the eternal mysteries that she should understand something about. Furthermore, it would scandalize Tiaa for her to be present at such a rough event, and she thought that anything she could do that might irk the forces of propriety—while she still had the chance—was worth a try.

Meret slipped out of her chambers as soon as she saw Tiaa nodding in a chair by a sunny doorway. Of course she would not go all by herself to the stables: her hairdresser Aset would go with her. Aset might be glad for a change of scenery herself.

With growing excitement Meret chattered as the two hurried along a portico that bordered the kitchen gardens. "I hope it's not all over by the time we get there, Aset. Do you think it will be?"

"No, Princess, these are not hasty matters. But let us hope, for the sake of all, that the birth does not take too long."

"Is it awfully messy? Will the horse scream? Oh, I won't be able to bear it if she suffers!"

"The horse will not enjoy it much, Princess, but that is the way it must be. She will be a good mother."

"I hope the men don't send us away. They had better not—" Rounding a shadowy corner, Meret nearly bumped into someone. Startled, she hopped back, stepping on Aset's toe, and peered at the intruder. Why, that young Greek again!

Before Meret could speak, Hector recovered from his own surprise and struck a pose with a swagger. "Princess Meret, what a pleasure to see you!" Then he caught sight of Aset, which threw him off for a moment. Nervously he adjusted the short cape he wore over a simple brown tunic.

"And what brings you here, sir?" Meret replied, attempting a properly haughty tone.

Hector quickly hid one hand behind his back. "I have business at the palace frequently, Princess Meret."

"In the kitchen gardens, too?"

At that, Hector relaxed a little and smiled. "Oh well, why pretend? You know I was really looking for you."

"Really!" said Meret, genuinely surprised by his directness. "But how did the guards let you enter, if you didn't have some message of great importance for the king's advisers?"

"Most of them know me by now," Hector said with a shrug of exaggerated confidence. "I tell them what they want to hear, and they let me pass. The advantages of official-dom. Princess, I've brought something for you. Do you want to see it?"

Meret hesitated. The horse was still on her mind—but the afternoon had suddenly taken on a different aspect. She turned to Aset. Would the servant interfere with this unexpected and not-quite-proper encounter? No, Aset stayed in the shadow, hands demurely clasped, face impassive.

Maybe Meret could linger — at least long enough to find out what gift a Greek might think fit to bring her.

"All right," she said, "what do you have?"

With a grand gesture, Hector brought his hidden hand forward. It clutched an odd-looking object like a large spherical wooden flower covered with half-open coarse petals. "Look!" he said proudly. "It comes from a tree, a kind of pine that grows on the mountains of the Lebanon. And inside each of these little petals there's a nut with a delicious kernel. One of the lieutenants who's just come from Tyre brought a whole sackful for my father. He dotes on them."

The idea of the great military commander doting on tiny nuts amused Meret. It reminded her of her own father's passion for a certain kind of white grape . . . and how she loved to feed them to him one at a time, when they were in privacy. Who would care for him lovingly, knowing his little quirks and cravings, if she should have to leave? With effort, she set aside the thought and looked more closely at the strange object from across the sea. What a peculiar gift for a princess! It gave off a curious fragrance, sharp but sweet. She picked a brown kernel from a half-opened petal and lifted it to her mouth.

"Not that way, Princess!" said Hector with a laugh. "I don't want you to break those pretty teeth. Here, sit down, and I'll crack you some."

All thoughts of the horse slid from Meret's mind as she seated herself on a wooden bench and watched eagerly. Hector squatted nearby on the stone paving and, with the handle of his dagger, pounded the seed until it cracked open. Sure enough, inside lay a little white kernel. Nibbling it, Meret found it had a mild but pleasing flavor.

"Good!" she said. "Give me another."

Hector cracked a few more of the hard shells and handed her the kernels, which rested on his palm like tiny white fish. Then impulsively he stretched out his hand toward the silent, standing Aset. She stepped forward, accepted the kernel, and retreated to a bench a short distance away.

Noticing, Meret felt a flicker of adventure. If Tiaa or anyone else had come with her, she thought, the Greek would be halfway to his barracks by now.

She focused her attention again on Hector's gift. "So this is the treasure you bring me from the land of the Phoenicians. Ah, but we Egyptians discovered the wonders of that country long ago. Did you know that? Our kings have been bringing the famous cedarwood of the Lebanon since—oh, thousands of years. I have read about it. I know all about the days when Egypt ruled those fabulous cities as if they were"—she had to think of a good phrase—"hounds at the master's chair."

For a moment Hector looked slightly chastened, but he quickly recovered the initiative. "And so you did, you Egyptians. But have you, Princess Meret, ever seen those fabulous cities with your own eyes?"

Meret shook her head.

"Well, then!" said Hector, sitting cross-legged and looking up at her. "You cannot imagine how different that land is from Egypt. It's a beautiful country, with majestic, snow-topped mountains rising from the shore. And the cedars are truly magnificent, as big as—as pyramids. As for the Phoenicians themselves—by Zeus, they are rich! Shrewd traders, clever and intelligent, you can't get anything past them. But . . . they're a strange people."

"How so?"

"Some of their ideas. Their religion—*very* strange. They believe their gods demand terrible sacrifices. Young children! They burn their own children for their gods! It's true—I was told about it more than once."

Meret recoiled with a gasp. "Oh, I'd never heard *that*. True gods could never be that cruel."

Glancing up at her with one eyebrow cocked, Hector said, "No? Then tell me about your gods."

A challenge! But she liked being forced to think about something that nobody ever questioned. Ordinarily, only her father ever goaded her to debate.

"I believe," she said thoughtfully, "that religion is beautiful, that it shows us how to lead good lives and please the gods. The gods keep the world as it should be, and so they must be good. Our priests take care of the gods, and . . . and it all works very nicely."

"That's really what you think?"

"Yes," Meret answered, but with a tiny pause.

"Then," Hector said, "you have never seen men dying in battle. You have never seen women and children in the aftermath, whole families slaughtered . . . for nothing."

No, she hadn't. But she had read stories of battle, and something deep within told her that behind even the most glorious accounts of Egypt's military might, there was another reality. She must try, nevertheless, to salvage something of her views.

"That's true," she said. "I spoke too simply. The gods can't prevent all disaster. But what else can we believe? What can the simple people believe? Isn't it best for them to trust that the gods will always take care of them? I think that's better than living in fear all the time."

Hector was silent, and it looked to Meret as though he were debating whether to pursue the subject any further. Then, giving one more pine seed a whack with the handle of his dagger, he said, "I suppose there's some good in all religions. But if you ask me, there's more that's bad."

"Then what do *you* believe?"

"Hmm." Hector put down his knife, got to his feet, and leaned against one of the white-plastered pillars of the portico. He spoke thoughtfully. "I value the ideas of our great poets and thinkers, who speculate about the world and how men relate to the gods and to each other."

"Men only?"

He smiled. "Women don't have to think about such matters." Before Meret could retort, Hector went on, his voice taking a more probing tone. "But I've heard something recently about your Egyptian religion . . . that there's one woman who is actually believed to be *married* to a god. Is that true?"

Meret stiffened. Must that subject be dragged in and spoil their pleasant time? "I suppose you mean the Divine Wife," she said cautiously. "Consort of the great god Amun."

"Yes, something like that. Doesn't it strike you as rather an odd idea, that a human can be the wife of a god?"

Meret answered in a dry, matter-of-fact voice. "It started a long, long time ago—and you must know by now that we Egyptians love to hold on to ancient things. The Divine Wife helps the great Amun to keep Egypt fertile and prosperous. But more than just that."

"Oh?" Hector asked in a tone both curious and skeptical.

"She can help in other ways, too. The great king Psamtik, more than a hundred years ago, made his daughter the Divine Wife—I think she was just my age—and it helped unite the whole country under his rule. The Divine Wife and her priests have a great deal of power, you see. They must be loyal to Pharaoh. If they are not, if they wish to oppose his rule . . ."

"I do see," said Hector. "Well, I guess maybe it's all right for the god to have a priestess for his wife, if he really needs one. But I've heard that the next Divine Wife is supposed to be a young girl. Is it . . ." He hesitated a moment. "Is it true that a princess, or some other girl of noble birth, is going soon to Thebes?"

Meret turned to one side. Picking at some of the pine nut shells on the bench beside her, she wondered how to put him off. "It's true," she finally answered, feeling his gaze intent upon her. "You must remember, the Divine Wife is the richest and most powerful woman in Egypt."

"Really? Even more than the queen?"

"Egypt has no queen."

Hector's eyebrows went up. "I thought Pharaoh had many wives."

"Wives, yes," answered Meret, "but no queen. He has to have many wives, to keep good relations with other noble families in Egypt and with the kings in Asia. But he has not had a queen since . . ."

When she paused, Hector prompted again, "Yes?"

"Since my mother left us for her eternal home," Meret said quietly. She had long wondered whether her father would ever want to make another woman his queen, but so far he had shown no sign of it. Her mother apparently still held a unique place in his life, and that gladdened Meret's heart.

A moment passed before Hector murmured, "I understand."

Did he, too, know what it was like to grow up without a mother? Meret felt a delicate thread start to pull her toward him.

Before either could speak again, a servant girl approached with tiny, quick footsteps. She bowed low and murmured a message. Meret then turned to Hector. "Someone from the Greek camp has come for you."

With a sigh, Hector got to his feet. He picked up the bristly cone and handed it to Meret. "Next time," he said, "I shall bring you something more elegant. Some verses by our

great poet, Homer, which I copied onto papyrus—to see if
Greek ideas would flow onto an Egyptian writing surface.
Just to show you that we Greeks are not all barbarians."

"I never said you were," said Meret, blushing.

"I can read Egyptians' thoughts even though I have not
yet mastered their writing." Hector smiled and took Meret's
hand. She barely had time to be shocked when she found
that their hands were stuck together. Pulling hers away, she
saw smears on her palm.

Hector laughed. "Resin, from the pine tree. That's the
price you pay for its fruit. Your hand will take a bit of scrub-
bing—but it'll help you remember me." He turned with a
military flourish, and was gone.

Meret smelled the resin on her hand. It's like him, she
thought. Pungent yet somehow appealing. And tenacious,
indeed.

Aset approached. "Princess," she murmured, "the hour
is late now. The respected Tiaa will be looking for you."

Still musing, Meret returned to her chambers. She did
not think again about the mare until, at her evening meal,
one of the servants reported that Pharaoh's stables had
increased by the addition of a healthy little filly that afternoon. Then Meret felt annoyed that she had missed it. But
she was not sorry for the way the day had turned out.

CHAPTER 5

The sun god was already on his nightly journey by the time Bata reached Ipu's tavern. Work in the shop had kept him busy longer than usual, sweeping and cleaning and helping to pack the finished pieces for delivery. Then, too, knowing it would not be proper to meet the Greek as he was, covered with sweat and stone dust, he had stopped to rinse off at a large earthenware jar of water in the alley.

He found himself in a dejected mood, brought on by the uneasy atmosphere in the workshop. Previously, the men had been neither unkind nor particularly friendly. Sometimes he thought they might feel that Smendes favored him more than a clean-up boy deserved . . . especially a boy from the street, with no family. But since the Greeks' two visits, the men had turned almost hostile. Their dour faces clashed with the beauty they were creating.

And now this Greek. Maybe he was just playing games with an ignorant boy. Or perhaps the gods were playing games. Bata believed the gods were benevolent . . . but now he wondered: could they sometimes take pleasure in toying with people's lives?

Arriving at the tavern, Bata peered around nervously until, by the light of the smoky oil lamps, he spotted the Greek at a small table in the farthest corner. Hector motioned to Bata to sit down and pour himself some beer from a half-empty jug.

"They kept you working late?"

"Because of the special order for the palace. We must have everything ready in a day or two."

"Yes, I've learned something about all that," said Hector curtly. "But I'm not interested in talking about it."

He looked glum, and Bata wondered whether Hector was one of those men who became gloomy with beer, rather than happy. Feeling it was his place to follow a lead rather than start a conversation, Bata waited patiently for a minute or so.

At last Hector spoke again, still reserved. "The work in your shop is very good. I've never seen such stone vessels, carved almost as thin as ceramic. They must be the best in Egypt. But some of the other things—" He caught himself, then burst out in a torrent, "I don't understand how you Egyptians think! Your religion, I mean. It's not just because you have so *many* gods—everyone does. Except the Hebrews, and they're an odd bunch any way you look at them. But why do you worship animals? That's so *unnatural*. Look, we Greeks have plenty of deities, a lot more than we need, if you ask me. But at least they're in human form, as they should be. And they're beautiful to look at, natural, *true*. But you Egyptians, you worship the impossible, the ugly! Why do you believe in such creatures?"

Bata was stunned. His own suspicions of the gods, which had troubled him just a short while earlier, dissolved. How could he answer this arrogant Greek, who was clearly waiting for a reply? At last he managed to say the only thing that came into his head. "Because they are our gods. They've been our gods since before the beginning of time.

How could they not be true? Why shouldn't we believe in them?"

Hector snorted and took a long gulp of beer. "The world changes," he said, "and you hang on to your old gods simply because you've always had them. If Egypt wants to be strong, you people will have to learn to think differently. You have to use your minds, use *reason*. That's what our great thinkers tell us. You can't go on believing the impossible, just because people did a thousand years ago."

Once again, Bata could do nothing but stare. Why, the Egyptians' gods had kept the world going for countless ages. Now, with the country so prosperous, surely that was all the proof needed that the gods were doing just fine. Wasn't it? And as for *reason*, what on earth did *that* mean? Bata hadn't the faintest notion what Hector was talking about.

In fact, he felt totally confused. First Hector said he wanted to understand what Egyptians believed, then he announced that they were dead wrong. And yet Bata found himself wanting to grasp what the Greek was trying to tell him.

Hector went on. "For instance, those sphinxes in your master's workshop. Excellent work, but . . ."

"Those are not gods. They just show how strong Pharaoh is, like a lion."

"Oh. All right, then. But the statue your master is working on—that's a god, isn't it? He's creating a masterpiece, so far as the carving goes. But it's incredibly ugly! Why should anyone want to worship something so ugly?"

Bata gasped. "Please, no—you don't understand! That is Taweret, just as she is. My master Smendes simply shows her truly, so that anyone who sees the statue will know who she is and be reminded of her goodness. No, Taweret could not possibly be ugly."

With a grimace, Hector shook his head as if the whole idea were incomprehensible. A moment later his face softened.

"All right, maybe I shouldn't have said what I did. I don't mean any harm. But it baffles me to see people willingly deceive themselves, when all they have to do is open their eyes and start asking questions. Including you, Bata."

Ask questions—about the gods? What an amazing notion! But somehow it pricked at him, tempted him in a way he'd never experienced before. Anyway, why should it matter what he thought, and why should this Greek care in the least about what went on in his heart? Right now, in fact, his heart felt confused, and the part that did his thinking wasn't working very well. He certainly wasn't ready to ask any questions. The beer was making him dizzy—he'd had little to eat that day. He was glad to see Hector call the tavern keeper for some freshly baked bread and half a roasted duck.

As the two ate and drank, Bata felt a pleasant warmth overcome his tension and weariness. They talked—they even laughed—and Hector's glum mood seemed to pass. Unlike the other apprentices and laborers who were the only young people Bata knew, Hector had interesting things to talk about. He had lived in foreign places, observed the strange customs of the people. To an Egyptian they were barbarians, those Phoenicians, Hebrews, Babylonians, Philistines, but they did make for some good stories.

And Hector could even laugh at himself. "You know, Bata," he said at one point, "names are funny things. I don't know if yours means anything, but mine . . . do you know what mine means? No, of course you don't. I was named after a great warrior. Hector, hero of Troy. A great warrior." He laughed loudly and slapped the table.

Wondering what the point was, Bata said, "Well, that's good for the son of a warrior, isn't it?"

Hector's grin faded. "Exactly. But what do I do? Fight? No. I talk. I study and listen to other people, and then I talk.

I've witnessed *one* battle—from a distance. That's all my father wants me to do."

"But," Bata said, "do you really want to fight? Do you really want to see men killed, and kill men yourself?"

After a moment's pause, Hector said almost fiercely, "I want a chance to prove my courage, my strength. I don't want to be forever kept on the side—the general's precious son who must be protected from all harm."

Bata found it hard to keep up with Hector's rapid changes in mood. It was something like rounding up a flock of frightened ducks in the marketplace. He stammered, "But you do other things that are more important . . . don't you?"

Hector sat slumped, then straightened up and let out a sigh. "Yes, it is important, the talking, I guess, and I'm useful enough, I suppose. Except when I'm doing stupid things like filching figs in the street. I just wish . . . I could really be a hero. Wish I didn't feel like a horse that's trained for battle but is kept in the stable."

"I think," said Bata hesitantly, "I understand."

"Do you? I don't see how you could."

At that, Bata kept his thoughts to himself. Being a hero was something he could hardly care less about, especially if it meant yelling and waving a sword and hacking other people's arms off. In fact, he doubted that Hector really wanted to do all that. . . . But Bata knew about his own feelings, his yearning to do something beautiful the way his master did—all the while knowing that he couldn't. It did give him, he thought, a little glimpse into Hector's soul.

Suddenly Hector broke the moment's silence. "Anyway, right now . . . right now I am going to do something very important. I shall call for another jug of beer!"

He laughed, and although it sounded strained, it was better than the bitterness that had twisted his mouth a few moments earlier. Relieved, Bata tried to make a joke, and soon Hector's humor seemed completely restored.

As the jug got emptier, Bata began to notice something else. Hector wasn't doing *all* the talking. The dizziness past, Bata found himself starting to talk with more confidence. He, too, had things to say, things he'd never even suspected might be hiding in his heart. He heard himself talking about his work and his devotion to the irritable old man who had found him in the street, barely old enough to walk, and had taken him in and brought him up. He spoke of his longing to do *something* good. And Hector listened, watching him, often asking him to repeat a word or explain a phrase.

Yes, thought Bata, beer might not be good for his old master's heart—but it could be quite splendid for a young man's!

CHAPTER 6

"Come, daughter," said Ankh-haf, pharaoh of Egypt and father of the god Amun's future wife. "Let us walk now in the twilight, before the stinging insects find us. There are many things we have to talk about, and I'm afraid there will not be another chance before your departure."

Meret scowled, taking care to bend over and fuss with her sandal strap so her father would not see. She had no desire to hurt him, but every reminder of what lay ahead revived pangs of dread and panic. If only she could *think* . . . find some new argument to persuade him that she could serve him better here than in the Sacred City.

They entered the largest of the palace gardens and strolled along a pathway inset with designs in marble. Alongside the path, branches hung heavy with crimson pomegranates. A bird twittered among the fronds of a tall date palm.

Neither Meret nor her father spoke for a few minutes. She recalled the many other evenings they had strolled in the gardens together, before her mother left them for the eternal land in the West. In those days her parents had let

her explore freely, as if the whole palace were her play-
ground. But now the happy moments were all in the past.

As they drew near a rectangular pool that lay among
stands of tall ornamental grasses, a fish leapt high, then fell back.
The unseen splash roused Meret, and she spoke abruptly.

"That fish will spend its whole life swimming circles in
that pool. And it's more fortunate than I am."

Ankh-haf looked at her with curiosity. "What do you
mean by that, my daughter?"

Returning his look, Meret said, "Why, my father, that
fish has the freedom to be itself, to do what is natural for it.
Frankly, I'd like to jump into the pool with it right now and
spend the rest of my life happily swimming in circles."

Her father let out a sound halfway between a chuckle
and a snort of annoyance. There, she had done it again,
Meret thought. She seemed destined to say such silly things
that no one could take her seriously.

Reaching the farthest end of the garden, they paused
under an arbor. Bunches of purple grapes hung only a few
inches above Pharaoh's head. There was no one in view.
Guards stood discreetly along the wall but out of sight among
tall flowering plants, and Ankh-haf had dismissed the three
servants who ordinarily accompanied him around the palace.
Meret had a good idea why.

At last he spoke, keeping his voice low. "I'm not sure
whether you fully understand, my daughter Meret, how
much the future of the Two Lands depends on you."

"Oh, Father. You have told me, and Tiaa has told me,
and so has everyone in the whole palace—everyone who
dares tell me *anything*. And I still don't want to go to the
Sacred City and spend the rest of my life there, owning half
of Egypt and living like a prisoner." Now Meret did not try
to conceal the misery on her face. This was her last chance to
speak to her father openly.

"A prisoner," said Pharaoh musingly. "A strange thought, for one who will be the most powerful woman in the land—in any land. But I have no intention of arguing with you, my daughter. We have been over this ground before."

"Then why, beloved Father," asked Meret, trying to calm her voice, "did you want to talk with me tonight?"

"Because I want you to understand fully why your role in the Sacred City is so critical for the future of your country—and for my future."

The changed quality of his voice, somber in a way she had not heard before, caught Meret's attention. She noticed, too, with new concern, the thinness of his face, the worry lines and marked pouches under his eyes. She listened more closely.

"Possibly you already have an idea," Ankh-haf went on. "But there must be no uncertainty at all in your understanding, because even the slightest lack of resolve on your part could bring disaster."

The western skies were rosy now. The garden had sunk into the silence of night, broken only by the song of a nightingale. But the idyllic moment was wasted on Meret. Alarmed by her father's words, she waited for him to continue.

Ankh-haf took a few aimless steps, his head low. Then he stopped and turned toward his daughter. "Egypt prospers, Meret. The gods have cared for us, and for many years the land has been fruitful. But even in the finest fruit, a tiny worm may lie at the center, a worm that can grow until nothing is left within—but rot." His voice dropped almost to a whisper. "I have done everything I can to make Egypt powerful, strong enough to keep all enemies at bay. But I fear a worm within. Jealousy, resentment, ambition . . . they are that tiny worm, feeding upon itself, always growing larger. And in time, that worm becomes a monster . . . the monster called treachery. Betrayal."

The dim light of torches along the path revealed the bitterness of Ankh-haf's expression. He went on. "In the days of our great kings of the past—Thutmose, Seti, Ramses— Egyptians had a fighting spirit. In our times, I fear, it seems that we Egyptians would rather enjoy the sun, full stomachs, and empty chatter."

His voice took on a tone almost sarcastic. "And now, suddenly, the mood is changing. Suddenly our military leaders feel an ardent love for martial glory. Or so they claim. They don't want our friends from the far islands to be the core of Egypt's fighting force—they want to do it themselves."

Yes, thought Meret, *I've noticed some of those generals— lazy Akunosh, fat old Harwa. They complain and criticize the Greek mercenaries, and talk of their own military prowess, when they're really just all bluster—and too much wine on the side. But what is my father trying to tell me?*

Pharaoh turned back to his daughter. "Not only is the army, with its hostility between Egyptian and Greek, a worry to me. The reports I receive from the Sacred City grow more disturbing with every month. Can I count on the loyalty of my troops there? What about that all-powerful priesthood? I am no longer sure, my daughter. It has happened before in Egypt's history that the Sacred City in the south rivaled and even overpowered Pharaoh in the north. But I must keep Egypt united. I must use every means possible to have the entire Two Lands of Egypt at my back. Not just in case of war, but to remain Egypt's king!"

"But, Father—"

Ankh-haf cut her off. "Yes, it has come to that. My own throne is in danger. So you see, my daughter, I must find a sure way to unite the Two Lands. And there is no surer way than by having the royal princess established in the Sacred City as the Divine Wife of Amun."

Meret shivered. She knew about the threat from the east,

the Persian war machine that had rolled over so many lands. She had sat in on more than one tense meeting with Pharaoh's military advisers—and rumors floated through the palace like the smell of cooking onions from the kitchen. But the king's suspicions of disloyalty, even treachery—both among his military commanders and in the Sacred City—all *that* was new to her. His words filled her with sudden dread.

"But . . . ," she stammered, "I don't understand what I can do. Egypt already has a Divine Wife, the revered Khnumut. You have explained to me what would happen. I would be the adopted daughter of the Divine Wife and, later on, the Divine Wife herself. Just the way it happened when the great Psamtik united Egypt by sending his daughter to be the next Divine Wife. But how can you be sure your plan would work in the same way?"

Ankh-haf replied in measured tones. "It is true that Khnumut still appears to be strong. And strong-willed. She holds on to every scrap of her lands—lands that could benefit all of Egypt and its people. By the gods, how she holds on! But enough of that. She has been the Divine Wife for many, many years now. However firmly she wields her power, she cannot reign forever. She must now prepare for her passing to the next life." His voice became harder. "That means she can no longer put off the adoption of her successor. She cannot go on forever resisting my wishes. This is the time for the next Divine Wife to be presented to her—and in such a way that she must accept."

Meret turned away to hide her alarm. The thought of having to leave her home and everyone dear to her was hateful enough. To be only a sort of apprentice forced upon Khnumut—possibly for several years—was a prospect even more distressing. What would the revered Khnumut be like, and how would Meret be treated during that period of waiting? It scared her to think of it.

At the same time, she recognized that her own worries were minor compared with her father's. No, she could not escape. She was the daughter of Pharaoh, destined to serve Egypt and Egypt's king to the best of her ability, just as if she were his son. Now it appeared that filling the role of Divine Wife was the only way. If her father's rule—or worse, his own safety—was really threatened, then she must do whatever she could. Duty, interests of state, and her love for him all demanded it.

"I understand, Father," she said quietly. "I will do as you wish." A wave of emotion gripped her. "But I will be so lonely!"

Ankh-haf laid a gentle hand on her arm. "You will not be alone, my beloved daughter. The goddess Taweret will be with you, always."

He embraced her, and then returned swiftly to the palace halls. Meret knew it was his way. Once he had secured agreement, there would be no further discussion. To think of it! After all these months of arguing and pleading, and in a moment she had given in so meekly! But what else could she do, now knowing the dangers he faced?

Alone with her thoughts, Meret stayed in the garden and sat on a stone bench by a pool, absent-mindedly arranging the cushions. She drew some comfort from what her father had said about the protecting presence of Taweret. But her heart pounded with a refrain: *Not fair, not fair!* Chest heaving, she sat rigidly, feeling as a captured cheetah must. She would do what she had to, for the sake of her father. But it was not fair!

CHAPTER 7

The next morning, Bata's evening in the tavern was a pleasant, woozy memory. It gave him something to smile about as he got to work in the shop.

Still, he felt vaguely troubled. What Hector had said about the Egyptians' gods . . . maybe Bata *should* think about it. Hector was obviously very smart. He knew a lot more than Bata could ever hope to. Besides, it was the first time anybody had ever told Bata to think about anything at all, and he found the idea interesting.

Maybe he should talk with Smendes. Smendes would know. And certainly nobody but Smendes would listen to him.

The master was still working hard on the statue, always finding some tiny flaw that must be made perfect, then polishing and buffing till the fine stone seemed to glow with inner life. Sometimes Bata saw a shaft of light fall upon the statue from an opening in the reed roof above, and as the sunbeams shifted, it almost appeared as though the statue, too, were moving. At such moments Bata had the fanciful notion that the goddess was straining to come alive.

Yet he worried, because Smendes did not seem able to finish his creation. The tail in particular was still attached too thickly to the back. And there could be no further delay: the men from the palace were coming for the entire collection of pieces that very night. Princess Meret was leaving for the Sacred City the next morning.

Why couldn't the master finish the statue? Every man in the shop worried and muttered. Bata saw them casting apprehensive glances toward Smendes and his creation. But on he worked, perfecting small details, never hurrying.

After a while the master laid down the polishing tool and then lowered his frail body onto a rough bench. His breath came heavily, and he seemed utterly exhausted. Bata, hoping some food would revive his strength, brought him a small jug of beer and a broiled breast of duck.

At last the old man spoke. There was no one closer, so Bata assumed the words were meant for him.

"You are afraid I will not complete the statue in time," said Smendes, his voice faint. "You need not be afraid. The gods tell me this will be my last creation, and therefore it must be my best. But I don't want it to be finished . . . because then I will be finished."

Had the gods really said that? Surely that could not be true! Bata drew back in dismay. Then he had an idea. Perhaps this was the time to question.

"Master," he said softly, "I know you are tired . . . but there is something I need to understand."

"What is it, boy?" Although the ancient voice seemed to come from a frightening distance, it was gentle.

"I'm confused, I'm all mixed up." Bata was aware that the other workers were watching him. It increased his uneasiness. He crouched at the old man's knee and spoke in a lower voice. "Master, you said the gods had told you the statue would — would be your last . . ."

"Yes? Speak up, boy."

"But, Master, could it not be . . ." Then Bata blurted it out. "Master, maybe what the gods said is not true! They could have made a mistake. Master, how do we know they are right? How do we know the gods are — are real?"

With a jerk, Smendes turned to him, the watery eyes suddenly alight, the frail body starting to tremble. "You question the gods, boy?"

Quailing, Bata stammered, "No! It — it's not I, but — but some people say — "

"*Some people?* The Greeks! You've been talking with that foolish young barbarian, that uncivilized puppy, that arrogant goat. I forbid it. It is not for you — not for any Egyptian — to question a god. What, do you want to bring down the gods' anger on all Egypt? Do you want to destroy the entire world? Not another word of this! Not another word, or I'll have you whipped!"

Bata jumped to his feet, staring in horror at the old man. He knew Smendes' temper, he knew Smendes' pain, and he knew Smendes' hatred of stupidity. But never had he heard the master rant like this. It was as if Bata's few groping words had gone spear-straight to the old man's heart, and now he was fighting like a harpooned hippopotamus — gravely wounded but still dangerous.

What could Bata say to calm his master? With unnatural strength the old man now perched upright on the edge of his seat, as though he might leap up and seize the boy. Helplessly, Bata fumbled for the words to ask forgiveness.

The next instant a tiny motion caught his eye. In his fear and shock, it seemed that he saw the statue move . . . a quiver of the heavy body, a glint in the large eye. Could it—? No, no, of course not! It was just Bata's agitated heart that deceived his senses.

Suddenly, Smendes struggled to his feet. His legs immediately buckled, and he tottered. Bata lunged to catch him, and the nearest workman leapt up as well. Then, with Bata still clumsily trying to hold him, the master dropped to the floor and lay still, facedown.

The men pushed Bata away and turned Smendes over onto his back. The old man's breath was coming rapidly. It seemed to Bata that the soul was struggling to leave the withered body. But Smendes' eyes opened and his gaze moved about, searching.

"It's clearer to me now . . . ," he whispered. "The gods have helped me to understand. The boy . . . where is the boy?"

Reluctantly, the men stepped aside and let Bata bend over him. Smendes slowly focused on the boy and with great effort forced out a few words, so faintly that Bata could barely hear.

"Finish my work, boy. The gods will help you . . ."

His face, just moments earlier distorted with pain and outrage, relaxed. It looked to Bata as though a little smile was smoothing out the wrinkled features. Then Smendes' eyes closed. He lay still, and Bata knew that the old man's heart was finally at rest in this world and preparing for the next.

What could his last words have meant? Bata seemed to hear their echo, but their meaning was beyond him. However much his own heart grieved, he could not help wondering why the master had chosen to put this impossible charge upon him.

CHAPTER 8

Less than a full day and night had passed since Meret's promise to her father that, for love of him, she would do as he wished. Yet she felt as though she had already moved on to a new life, leaving her years of freedom and happiness far behind.

In the afternoon sun she sat in a garden, one that adjoined the chambers where Pharaoh met with his advisers. It had no pool, only beds of lush green plants and a few date palms. Meret did not want to think about the happy fish that she had envied the preceding evening; she would forever associate *that* garden with her sad feeling of surrender.

She sat alone, except for the guards who stood at intervals along the wall. Tiaa had withdrawn tactfully when Meret told her and the other servants to leave. It made Meret recall glimpses of a softer, more understanding Tiaa, who might indeed share some of Meret's grief at having to leave her home.

Pharaoh was conferring with the Egyptian officers and those of the mercenary troops. She could hear the low murmur of their voices. It had often interested Meret to sit in on these discussions, trying to follow the talk of strategy and strengths, and her father had encouraged her interest. From now on, however, she would have nothing to do with military matters. That, too, was part of the old life.

Yet Meret couldn't stop herself from imagining the scene inside the chambers. More maddening, she found herself thinking of the young interpreter, Hector, who had brought her the pine cone from Mount Lebanon — and promised that he could be just as tenacious as its resin. Well, he was wrong. That meeting would be their last.

She heard a sudden rise in the men's voices. A dispute of some sort? No, it sounded as though the meeting had come to an end and people were leaving. The scuffing of feet in military sandals grew louder as the men left the chamber and walked along the portico next to the garden. On her bench, Meret shifted closer to some overhanging fronds that would partially shield her from view.

But suddenly someone stood before her, pushing aside the branches.

"Meret!" Hector exclaimed, his face flushed. "I knew you were here — I saw you through the window. I have to speak to you!"

Just like that! Bursting in on her like a lion and speaking as though he were addressing the cook!

Having caught his breath, Hector blustered on. "Is it really true? Are they really sending you away?"

"What do you mean by — by intruding like this? Your behavior is outrageous," she responded at last. She stood erect, with all the indignation she could command. If indeed she must be trained as the future Divine Wife, she would have to make her heart as firm as rock.

"Meret, listen — you must hear me!"

The audacity! Why, if it weren't that her father was doing everything possible to keep things smooth with the Greeks — why, she would call the guards instantly.

He kept right on. "I'm sorry—I know I shouldn't have taken you by surprise—" He flashed a nervous smile, for only an instant. "But I had to find out. Meret, what is going on? At first I didn't believe it when they told me you were going to Thebes. I thought—I *hoped*—it was somebody else. But now—is it true? Why didn't you tell me? Why did you conceal it?"

At his last words, Meret's heart felt pierced. Why hadn't she told him? Maybe it would have been better. It would have killed his interest in her quickly. But at that time she, too, had still clung to a shred of hope.

"You might have given me at least a hint," Hector insisted, when she did not answer. "How long will you be gone? When will you come back?"

Oh, as if she weren't miserable enough already! But now she must be hard—on him and on herself. Standing as straight as the palm trees nearby and keeping her voice as cool as the night winds, she spoke. "I will tell you only what you need to know, and then you must leave."

For the moment he was speechless. Meret continued without expression, her gaze fixed on a spot in the pebbled walkway.

"I have the great honor to be the next Divine Wife of the supreme god of the Sacred City, Amun. I shall soon leave with all ceremony, and I shall serve Amun as his consort for the rest of my days. That will be my life . . . and that is all I can say to you."

Hector took a step forward. "You can't do that! Not you, Meret!"

"It is determined. You must accept it, and you must never intrude on my privacy again."

At last Meret forced herself to look directly at the young Greek. Shocked by his expression of despair, for an instant she felt utterly stricken. Then, recovering, she clapped her hands and two tall guards appeared quickly. At the same moment, a Greek officer came striding into the garden. He reached Hector before the guards did and took the young man by the arm, while managing a quick bow to the princess.

Hector's eyes met Meret's once more, and then he was gone. The guards withdrew as quickly and silently as they had approached.

Alone, Meret raised her hands to her face. What had she done? She had been so cruel! Yet she had to be — to destroy all hope in him . . . and in herself.

Then, although she tried to shut it out of her mind, she saw his face again. His eyes . . . once lit by laughter, now dark with dismay. No, she must forget those eyes, and everything about the man they belonged to. From now on her attention would be directed only to the new life she must lead. All other thoughts and memories must remain behind her.

And besides, he was a Greek. Impossible. Everything was impossible. Everything.

CHAPTER 9

Bata arrived at the workshop early the next morning. In the soft gray light before dawn, the alley was still quiet.

The men had sent him away right after Smendes' death, cutting him off from a last view of the one person in the world who had cared for him. They didn't need to punish him—he blamed himself. If only he had been able to hold back his foolish question, Smendes might still be alive. Yes, it was surely his fault that the master had left this world so abruptly.

Bata had spent a long, wakeful night on the pile of straw in the cartmaker's shed where he slept. Tears trickling down his cheeks, he had cursed himself over and over, and wondered what would happen to him now. Could he go on working in the sculptors' shop under Hrihor, the overseer who would now take charge? Not likely. That man had never bothered to hide his disdain for Bata. He would have no sympathy for the one who had brought about the sudden death of the master—especially at such a busy time. No, Hrihor would undoubtedly tell Bata to go find some other work . . . if he could.

Meanwhile, Bata's heart ached with loneliness. Smendes, childless and unmarried, had been his only family. He had always been aware that behind the old man's sharp words lay a genuine desire to help the boy in life; it was the closest thing to affection that Bata had ever known. Thus his early morning return to the workshop had a ring of sad farewell, both to Smendes and to the place that had been home to him for as long as he could remember.

He found the rough wooden door ajar. Hrihor was already there, standing like a pyramid in the middle of a room now startlingly empty. He raised an eyebrow as Bata entered.

"So you've come back, boy. What did you expect to find today?"

"My—my regular work, I guess," stammered Bata.

"It's not a regular day, is it? Why should only you have regular work?"

Bata resisted the bait. Hrihor had always struck him as slightly ridiculous, strutting around the workshop with his gleaming belly shaking above the knee-length kilt that he wore as a badge of status. But until a new master carver came, Hrihor would have to be treated with deference.

Gazing around, Bata asked, "Did everything get delivered all right?"

"Yes. No thanks to you. It took till long after the middle of the night, but we met the palace orders."

"The sphinxes? Everything? And . . . and the statue of the goddess?"

A scowl came over Hrihor's plump face. "The statue of the goddess," he mimicked. "Of course not. Did you think we could send an imperfect work to the Divine Wife of Amun? Would that be worthy of the name of Smendes? The gods would curse us if we presented a statue in that state! What did you expect, you young fool?"

But the pedestal where the statue had stood for so long seemed to shout with emptiness. If the statue had not been delivered with the other goods, then where was it?

Hrihor went on. "It will never be finished. Only the hand of Smendes was worthy of that statue, and now that hand is gone. Along with the payment, I might add. And I hope the master's last words to you were a curse!"

Again Bata seemed to hear Smendes' last gasping words . . . far from a curse, but baffling. He could only trust that, in time, the meaning would become clearer. Right now, however, the statue's fate was what mattered, not his own.

"Where . . . where is — ?"

"It has been removed to the storeroom," said Hrihor coldly, "and there it will remain."

"Never to be seen again?" Bata's voice shrank almost to a whisper. That exquisite work, which had meant so much to the master, now shut up forever in a dark closet — ?

Hrihor merely tightened his lips, then took on a businesslike air. "Since you're here, you can get to work. The shop needs a good sweeping before the men arrive. Hop to it." He left, to take breakfast at a tavern.

Bata grabbed the broom and busied himself. With his head bent and eyes focused on the dirt floor, he could hide the tears if anyone should come in. He swept hard, releasing his misery in physical exertion. But as he bustled around in front of the closed door to the storeroom, he paused. Was there a sound coming from inside that dark, cramped space? A mouse? No, it seemed more like a sigh.

Oh, of course not! It was just the way he felt . . . so unhappy that the whole world, even the mice, seemed to be crying with him.

CHAPTER 10

All of Saïs, the splendid capital of Egypt, was in an uproar of celebration. From the palace windows, Meret saw hundreds of flags and banners whipping in the breeze and caught the murmur of thousands of excited voices. Not even the lowliest street sweeper would stick to his work this morning. The entire population was filling the streets, rejoicing for Egypt because the future Divine Wife was on her way to the Sacred City.

When the sun reached halfway to its noontime height, Meret started her stately procession from palace to river front, traveling aloft in a palanquin. Six husky young priests carried the golden poles that held a small platform piled high with cushions of luxurious fabrics. On the cushions rested Princess Meret in her pleated gown of finest linen shot with gold thread. Artfully applied cosmetics enhanced her features. Her jewelry—a collar and bracelets of gold, blue lapis, and turquoise—weighed enough to stagger a bullock . . . or so it felt. And a huge, elaborate wig concealed every bit of her own hair.

Gritting her teeth, Meret tried bravely to keep her head up. But the palanquin was a wobbly, scary thing to ride on at the best of times. Although the priests tried to walk in rhythm together, their steps kept falling out. When they snapped at each other for clumsiness, the jolts grew even worse. Meret kept a firm grip on the delicate railing along the sides of the platform, hoping she wouldn't go flying into the street if one of the bearers should stub his toe.

At least she didn't have to smile and look happy. Instructed to keep a sublime expression on her face, Meret endured her miserable trip in silence, seemingly oblivious to all the noise around her.

On any other festive occasion, she'd have been jumping up and down, stretching her neck to see everything, clapping her hands at the marvels on all sides. And there was so much to see! She could catch only an occasional view of the long procession that accompanied her, but she could certainly hear. Battalions of chanting, shaven-headed priests trudged beside her, wearing their leopard skins and other regalia. Troops of temple women tripped along cheerfully. Each one shook her tambourine or sistrum rattle as hard as she could, trying to make more of a din than her neighbors. Bands of male musicians added to the hubbub, all of them singing at the tops of their lungs, drowning out the efforts of the flutists.

And the dancing girls! Some of them, in long sheath dresses, were confined to stately maneuvers. Others, in almost nothing at all, went through acrobatic routines — backbends, leaps, splits — wherever the procession paused on a smooth surface. Catching a glimpse, Meret recalled how hard she had tried to do backbends as a young child . . . and how her parents had laughed and encouraged her.

Bringing up the rear was another army of priests. These men were struggling to hold erect the banners attached to long, heavy poles, insignia of the many separate provinces of Egypt whose unity would soon be happily confirmed by the betrothal of the princess from the north to the god in the south.

Everywhere along the way, people threw flowers. Half the blossoms in Egypt must have been plucked in her honor, Meret thought. But many were already trampled underfoot, and the sight revived her fears that she, too, would fade quickly in her luxurious prison.

Suddenly Meret's throat tightened: the procession was slowing as it passed in front of Pharaoh. In a garment dyed with purple from Tyre, her father sat on an elegant portable throne covered with beaten gold. Flanking him stood all his viziers, ministers, military commanders, and courtiers under large canopies striped in crimson and ivory. Meret bowed her head before him, then looked up and met his gaze across the distance. I shall never see him again, she thought. Her eyes filled with tears, which she tried desperately to blink away. Pharaoh's expression was stoical, but Meret could see sadness there as well.

Yes, Pharaoh, Meret thought, be sad to look upon your daughter for the last time. And may her sacrifice, made from love of you, keep Egypt strong.

Just then, like a willful spirit bent on causing her misery, another face seemed to intrude upon Meret's view of her father. The young Greek, his confident smile—and his despairing last look at her. Before the tears could spill and ruin her rouged cheeks, Meret willed herself to banish that image and focus instead on the gleaming shaven heads of the priests carrying her palanquin.

By the time the procession reached the dock, Meret had recovered her poise. She gasped at the sight of the royal barge, seeing it for the first time. No expense had been spared in creating a vessel in which she could travel in comfort on a voyage of sixteen days or more. Gleaming white sails of fine linen, not ordinary canvas, already huffed in the breeze. The cedarwood from which the entire craft was made gave off wafts of fragrance, even though it was completely painted in auspicious signs and trimmed with beaten gold.

A flotilla of lesser vessels decked out with flying banners would accompany the royal barge. The boats were laden with every possible provision that Meret and her flock of attendants would need. In addition, the fleet held a great supply of useless luxuries, all to impress her divine husband—and his priests—with the value of his next bride. Piles of ivory, gold objects without number, rare animal skins from Africa, silken robes from that unimaginably distant land to the east . . . the decks were laden. There was a pair of dwarfs—jugglers of astonishing skill—from the southern kingdom of Kush. There were four cheetahs declawed and desexed, a troop of trained monkeys, several identical black cats, and a bevy of whimpering greyhounds.

Yet the goods in these vessels were nothing compared with the value of the land and its produce to be bestowed on Meret as the consort of Amun. What would she do with it? She felt weary just thinking of it.

At last the princess and her attendants were safely on board. Suddenly, however, a flurry of new excitement broke through the continuous dancing, singing, and clapping. Something seemed amiss. Meret, settled on a high gilded seat, roused herself.

"What is it, Tiaa?" she asked her old nurse, who had taken a conspicuous position of importance nearby.

"Nothing, nothing at all, Princess Meret. Don't disturb yourself." Tiaa went on waving grandly to the crowd.

But for Meret, any little break in the monotony of rejoicing was welcome. It looked as though a man was arguing with the captain of one of the nearby vessels, and the two were getting more excited by the moment. What could be going on?

"Find out for me, Tiaa!" Meret ordered.

With an elaborate sigh, Tiaa told one of the young male servants to jump down to the dock and bring back the desired information. A short while later, he reported to Tiaa. She in turn reported to Meret, while the servant waited nearby, biting his lip.

"As I told you, Princess, it is nothing," said the nurse a bit waspishly. "A collection of fine stoneware has been delivered late, that's all, and now it's safely on board."

But the commotion on the dock was mounting. A noisy crowd had gathered around the two arguing men.

"Then what's all the fuss about?" asked Meret. Tiaa, obviously annoyed at having the perfection of her day rattled, made a quick gesture of dismissal. But Meret faced the young servant and demanded, "You, tell me. What is causing the trouble?"

Little more than a boy and on the scrawny side, the servant appeared awed half to death at being directly addressed by the future Divine Wife. "O your most ex—exalted highness, I understand that . . ."

"Yes? Go on!"

"They s-say that the pieces from the shop of the sculptor Smendes—they were not all delivered."

How silly, thought Meret. A bowl or vase unaccounted for, and they're making such a big fuss? She started to turn away, then took a closer look at the boy's face. He was clearly upset about something.

"Well? Just *what* is missing?" Meret could see that Tiaa and the other attendants were shocked at her talking directly to this servant, and it pleased her.

With lowered head and shuffling feet, the boy answered haltingly. "They say—" But before the words could come out, Tiaa clapped her hands loudly and gestured with her fan toward one of the men in charge of the boat. He stepped forward, laid a large hand on the skinny scruff of the boy's neck, and propelled him to another part of the vessel.

Meret glared at the nurse. "Tiaa, what do you mean by this? He was trying to tell me something."

"I mean," said Tiaa coolly, "not to let the babbling of an ignorant servant disturb the future consort of Amun. And not to let it throw any disorder into the perfection of our departure. The boy is clearly nervous and silly. He doesn't know anything, and you, my dear princess, have no business talking with him. Whatever the problem may be, let the servants take care of it. Now, let us compose ourselves for the last moments of ceremony."

Meret's anger subsided a little. She fought the pout that wanted to master her face, and soon restored her carefully painted features to something resembling serenity. Later she could inquire about the missing stone vases, or whatever they might be. There was plenty of time ahead. More than plenty.

CHAPTER 11

The world was spinning too fast for Bata. Yesterday had brought the terrible scene of the master's death and his own devastating sense of guilt. Today brought the most elaborate rejoicing Saïs had ever witnessed, to see the royal princess off on her glorious journey. Although Bata had not been allowed to attend the festivities, from the workshop he had certainly heard the noise—drums and trumpets, shouting and singing. But his heart was too heavy for celebration.

At the same time, an idea was growing inside that troubled heart. It pushed out other matters and absorbed his thoughts more and more as the day wore on.

Since work schedules were all thrown off, the sculptors' shop did not get back to business until after midday. By late afternoon Bata was still helping the carvers get ready for new projects. For the famed shop of Smendes, there was always a backlog of orders from the nobility and rich merchants.

Bata was so preoccupied with his idea that when he stepped out into the alley for a moment he hardly noticed the Greek soldier striding along—until the soldier deliberately

60

bumped into him. The man paused just long enough to mutter a message.

"Hector, son of Leander, awaits you at Ipu's tavern. Go there now." Then the soldier went on his way, with a more audible comment about "clumsy Egyptian sheep."

Hector wanted Bata to come to the tavern—*now*? What was he thinking of, more drinking and guffawing and making silly jokes about the gods? Well, he could just go on waiting. Bata wasn't interested.

As he went back to work, however, Bata could not dismiss the odd incident. Hector might be impulsive, but he was no fool. He knew that Bata had to work, and he would not have sent one of his father's soldiers with that message just for the fun of it. No, the more Bata thought about it, the more likely it seemed that Hector must have some serious purpose in mind.

At last he decided to take the chance and go. He would have to face the overseer's anger when he returned, but he was already used to that . . . his days in the workshop were numbered anyway. After dutifully cleaning some tools, he told Hrihor that he was going for a pail of water, then slipped out to the alley, ducked around the nearest corner, and ran.

The marketplace was still lively, because everyone had been at the docks all morning to watch the royal procession. Bata was scarcely aware of the hoarse shouting of the vegetable sellers, the smells of freshly slaughtered meat and hot cooking oil, the bleating of sheep and cackling of chickens. Intent on the idea taking shape in his heart, he waded through a flock of geese without even feeling their outraged nips on his bare legs, and he noticed too late a particularly oozy dropping from a cow. Well, the son of Leander would have to accept him as he was.

When Bata reached the tavern, he found Hector at the same small table in a corner. The other night, the two of them had not attracted much attention. Boys in their teens were frequent patrons of taverns. Bata feared, however, that at this time of day, when the place was not yet busy, they might be more conspicuous. He noticed the tavern keeper watching them with a puzzled frown on his heavy face. Then the man shrugged and went on trimming a bunch of green onions.

Another thing Bata noticed immediately: Hector was drunk. No doubt about it, he was already halfway under the table. And definitely not happy. He looked up, as Bata approached, with the eyes of a dying dog.

Disgusted, Bata sat down on the other stool. For this he had run off from work and would get a good beating to pay for it? Hector too soused even to talk? Yet Bata sensed that this was no ordinary drinking binge. The Greek appeared genuinely miserable.

Under the circumstances, Bata saw no need for special politeness. He spoke briefly. "I got your message, and I came. What do you want of me?"

Hector needed a little time to respond. At last he said, "I'm drunk, but not as much as you think. I . . ."

When he seemed to wrestle with his words, Bata said, "You what?"

"I . . . need some—somebody to talk to."

"Well, why me? You must know lots of Greeks you can talk to."

Hector gave a melancholy shake of his head, his gaze fixed glumly on the beaker between his hands. "No," he mumbled. "I can't talk to my father . . . he thinks I'm a . . . fool anyway. Can't talk to any of his officers, don't know anybody else. Can't let them see me like this. And I can't let them . . . know."

"Know what?" About his drinking in a lowlife Egyptian tavern? No, it seemed that Hector meant something more. "All right," said Bata, puzzled and annoyed. "But you didn't say why you wanted *me* to come."

"Because," said Hector bluntly, "you're safe. You don't matter."

Truth in drunkenness, thought Bata. I don't matter. He got up from the table and was about to walk away, when Hector stretched out a hand.

"Please. Wait." His voice was coarsened by drink, but he spoke with an uncharacteristic shyness that caught Bata's attention. "I mean, that's not all. It's because, also . . . I liked it the other time. I mean, talking with you. You don't know much, but you . . . understand."

Bata sat down again. No one had ever said anything like *that* to him before. "So," he said, "talk to me."

The Greek raised his head, sat up a little straighter, focused his eyes with effort, and really looked at Bata. Words suddenly seemed uncommonly hard for Hector. When they did come, they were surprising.

"No," he said thickly, "I better listen to somebody else for a while. Think about something else. Bata, tell me something in—interesting. Amuse me."

Fingering the edge of the table, Bata struggled inwardly. His heart was full of both the death of his master and the overwhelming idea that had been growing inside him. Could he talk about that idea? If he brought his plan into the open, would that give it life—or kill it? Well . . . he must take the chance.

At length, tight-throated, he spoke. "My master Smendes died yesterday. I caused his death. I didn't mean to, but I did. Now I must make up for it. I am going to do something for him."

Hector glanced up for a moment, with little interest, then looked down again. "Offerings. Prayers."

"No. I am going . . . ," Bata's voice gave out in a squeak. He swallowed and tried again, knowing that he must speak it all at once or it might never come out. "I am going to take his statue of the goddess Taweret to the royal princess in the Sacred City. My master made it for her, and he wanted her to have it. He knew she would need the protection of the goddess. No one else will take it to her, so I shall."

There. His idea, his amazing plan, was alive and in the world.

Hector suddenly looked as though he might fall off his stool. He gripped the table and stared at Bata, open-mouthed. When he found his voice, it was little more than a whisper. "You—you are going to—to Thebes? To the princess? But . . . how?"

Bata hadn't thought that far ahead. Reaching his big decision had been hard enough. He thought about it, and in a flash an answer came.

"Those coins you gave me—they'll pay for me to go on a cheap boat, won't they? Then in the Sacred City, after I've delivered the statue, I'll work until I can find a way to return to Saïs. I'm strong, I can find work."

As if a gust of fresh wind had blown the mist out of his mind, Hector sat up. His eyes, although reddened, were now focused and his mouth firm. It quite startled Bata to see this abrupt change. Had he said something wrong?

"No," said Hector. "You can't travel like that. Not lugging a val—valu'ble statue along. You'd be arrested in no time, or else it'd be stolen."

Dismayed, Bata realized the truth of what Hector had said. He hadn't thought of that, either. Would his great plan be demolished so quickly?

"There's a better way," Hector said. "I will go to Thebes, too."

Now it was Bata's turn to gape. *"You?* Why would *you* want to go to the Sacred City?"

The Greek ignored Bata's question and pondered for a moment. When he spoke, it was more as though he were talking to himself than to Bata. "I'll be on a special mission. Military information for my father. Yes. He needs all the information he can get. I'll pretend to be seeing the sights, the temples and everything, just visiting. Yes, that should work perfectly."

It sounded good to Bata, too. What did he know of such things? "But," he stammered again, "how does that—"

"Don't you see? Why, you'll be my servant. I can hardly travel without a personal servant to carry my things, can I? It's perfect, Bata."

The idea sank into Bata's heart and mingled with his own plan. Yes, it could work like that—yes! He had no objection to traveling as Hector's servant; serving was his lot in life. And he was glad to see the transformation from the sodden, morose Hector to the fired-up hothead he was more familiar with. Yet it was so odd, that sudden change in Hector, almost as though his thoughts had been on the Sacred City all along. Was it just the temples and wonders that he wanted to see, or did he have something else in his heart?

"Yes," Bata said slowly, "I think it will be a good plan. But why, Hector, do you want so much to go to the Sacred City?"

The Greek let out a big sigh, then fixed Bata with an intense stare. "Will you promise to say nothing—not a word? To anybody, ever?"

With a hand over his heart, Bata gave his solemn promise.

Hector dropped his gaze again. "All right, I'll tell you," he said in a low but fervent voice. "Because I'm in love with the princess Meret. And I'm damned if I'll let her be married to that god! No, not to Amun—or anyone else!"

• • •

All the way back to the shop, Bata mulled over Hector's astonishing declaration. What an idea—that the Greek could prevent the royal princess from becoming the future wife of the great Amun! Improper, impious, dangerous! Why, if the god were denied his rightful consort, he would surely be angry—and then what might happen to Egypt?

At the time, Bata had been too shocked to do more than listen dumbly to Hector's plans for their departure. Now, however, he felt the need to work out a reasonable way of looking at the whole thing. On the one hand, he couldn't help feeling alarmed; but on the other, he certainly did not want to lose this unexpected chance to make the journey with ease.

Finally Bata decided not to try to dissuade Hector from his outlandish scheme. The Greeks had strange notions, and Hector seemed particularly good at defying common sense. Well, let him think what he liked for now: he would have to face the truth sooner or later. Besides, it was possible that the Greek gods had a hand in Hector's seeming madness. Bata knew nothing about those gods; maybe they were mischief-makers. In any case, he thought it prudent not to give them any cause to take offense.

At the same time, the thought of his conversation with Hector brought a bitter twinge to Bata's heart. Wrapped up in his own concerns, the Greek had responded with indifference when Bata told him about Smendes. Hector knew how much Smendes had meant to Bata, for Bata remembered telling him. Yet he had not offered the least condolence. Surely he could have said *something*.

By the time Bata reached the stone carvers' shop, his thoughts had settled down somewhat. Yet his heart was so full of these thoughts and the afternoon's events, he hardly noticed it when Hrihor welcomed him with a good cuff on the ear and several whacks on the rear end with a broom.

"There!" shouted Hrihor with a last wallop. "That'll teach you to skip off in the middle of the afternoon. And don't think we're done with it. You stay here tonight after everyone has left, and when I arrive in the morning, I expect to find this place as clean as Pharaoh's bed. Not a crumb of stone anywhere, not a tool out of place. I don't care if it takes you all night."

This woke Bata up, and he looked around. The shop was a mess. Normally the men tidied up somewhat as they worked, but today they had apparently been told not to bother: let the boy clean up everything, teach him a lesson. Bata knew it would take him hours to sweep every chip from the dark corners and to wipe off the stone dust that flew everywhere when a piece was being turned on the wheel.

As soon as the stone carvers left, he got to work in earnest. The overseer was the last to depart. As Hrihor waddled out, Bata had a fierce urge to use the broom on the man's own fat rump, but he resisted it. He wanted no more trouble. Besides, he wanted to think about his plan again. As he did so, his mood turned almost jubilant.

His great idea had indeed burst into life! He was truly going to the Sacred City, taking the statue of the goddess directly to the princess. *That* was how he could carry out his master's wishes.

Now he must consider the details, such as how he would get that heavy statue out of the shop without being caught. The problem had stumped him earlier—but thanks to Hrihor, he now had the perfect opportunity. When he finished work late in the evening, he could take the statue with him. Wait. Could he lift it by himself? Three men had been needed to carry the original block, and the statue was still a sizable chunk of unusually dense stone. How could Bata drag it through the streets without attracting attention, or even breaking it?

The waning moon was high when Bata at last finished cleaning up the shop. His eyes burned from strain—only one small oil lamp had been left for him—but he felt he'd done the best job he could. At last he could sit down and eat the gritty barley bread and onions that Hrihor had grudgingly provided. Again he thought of Smendes, who had always made sure the boy was well fed and warmly clothed in the damp chill of winter.

When he felt revived, Bata headed for the small, cluttered storage room. Only one long day had passed since he'd last seen the statue, yet somehow the time seemed much longer. He felt a yearning . . . the statue had meant so much to his master. Bata remembered watching Smendes perfecting each detail, so absorbed he seemed to be guided by some divine presence within the stone.

He pushed open the rough, creaking door—and caught his breath. Although the statue had been pushed into a corner, a shaft of moonlight from a small opening overhead fell directly upon it. The pale highlights and deep shadows gave the statue the appearance of a living being. What miraculous work the master had done!

And then Bata saw the head turn.

Impossible! What tricks were his eyes playing on him? Oh, it was nothing . . . he just couldn't see straight because he was so tired. He groped to hold on to something steady. And at that moment a faint voice reached him.

"At last you have come . . ."

The voice sounded as though it had not been used in a long time. Bata stared, his eyes bulging. The statue had moved—the statue had spoken! Was it possible? No, of course not.

"Don't be alarmed . . . ," came the voice again. "And don't just stand there, please. This place is quite disagreeable."

Bata blinked and rubbed his tired eyes. He tried to speak, but nothing would come out.

"Come, young Bata," said the statue more firmly. "A deity must often be patient, mortals being as they are, but I have been waiting long enough."

Those words struck some sense into Bata. They seemed to call for an apology, and he must respond. Trembling, at last he managed to say something. "I'm sorry . . . I had to clean the whole shop first. Because I was . . ."

"I understand. Now, will you take me away from here?"

"Yes, that's just what I'm planning to do."

As soon as the words were out of Bata's mouth, he nearly staggered with amazement. He was speaking to the statue — no, to the *goddess Taweret!* For he knew just as surely as he had ever known anything in his life that he was looking at the goddess, and she was real. Somehow, the statue had become Taweret herself and she was speaking to him — to Bata, a simple, ordinary boy.

Oh, Smendes was right, so right!

The goddess spoke again. "Tell me of those plans." Her voice was growing clearer, and now she sounded almost eager.

Bata gulped twice, but the words, once he got started, came easily. "I'm going to take you to the royal princess in the Sacred City. Because you weren't — weren't done in time and the men wouldn't let you go. But I know Smendes wanted it very much, so I'm going to do it for him. So that you can protect the princess."

"Excellent," said the goddess. "Let us be on our way."

"Yes, of course." Bata was still shaken but thrilled. "As soon as Hector makes arrangements for the voyage. But I'm afraid I'll have to hide you somewhere, until we're ready to go. I hope it won't be too long. I — " He stopped, suddenly realizing that his wretched corner of a toolshed was no place for a goddess. "I'm afraid I don't know where to keep you. I was going to hide the statue where I sleep, but now . . ."

"Let us not worry about that. A deity must also be tolerant at times, and I'm sure you will do your best to make me comfortable. The important thing is to get out of this storage closet and on our way to the Sacred City." The immense mouth of the goddess widened and her bulbous eyes gleamed as she spoke.

Still Bata hesitated, shuffling awkwardly. Everything would be hopeless if he could not lift the goddess. And what would happen if he should drop her? He stammered, "I-I don't know if I can—"

"Ease your worries, young Bata," said the goddess. "You will find that while I am still closely associated with the excellent stone that the good Smendes chose for my earthly representation, I do retain powers that affect my form and attributes. Such changes may surprise you now and then, but there is no cause for concern. I shall try not to be too great a burden for you."

Ah, she understood what was in his heart, without his even having to express it. Although he had only partially grasped the sense of the deity's speech, he trusted completely . . . for why should he doubt any detail of this miracle?

He searched around the storeroom and found a length of ragged old linen. Hardly daring to touch her, he managed to wrap it around the goddess, then tried to lift her. To his surprise, although she stood almost as high as his arm was long, she was not so heavy as he had feared. He carried her from the storage room and out of the shop, setting her down briefly to shut and bolt the doors behind him. When he lifted her again, it was easier. Maybe, he thought, he was just getting used to the weight. Or could she be helping him by somehow becoming lighter?

All the way to the cartwright's toolshed, down one dark alley and up another, Bata found his steps speeded by the words singing in his heart. *It is true, it is true! The gods are real, and they can do anything! Taweret talks to me, and she lets me talk to her. Could anything be more wonderful? Surely my plan will succeed — and I will finish the master's work.*

CHAPTER 12

In the excitement of the actual departure, when all ropes were at last cast off, the sails starting to fill, and the fleet of golden boats moving out into the river, Meret forgot about the strange scene on the wharf. Her feelings were such a jumble—sadness and resentment, mingled with awareness of her unique importance to her father. And yes, she admitted to a tiny bit of curiosity about what the coming days might bring. For a while her heart had no room for anything else.

Once she settled down, however, she recalled the men arguing on the dock and the young servant who had tried to tell her something before being whisked away. Again Meret felt angry at Tiaa's bossiness. As they were eating their mid-day meal, she decided to pursue the matter.

"Tiaa," she said, disarmingly sweet, "I want to know what the problem was, just before the boats were ready to leave. You shooed away the boy before he could tell me, and I have a right to know these things."

The nurse gave a little huff, but a worried look flitted into her eyes. "As I told you, Princess, it was a mere nothing.

Nothing you need concern yourself with. That's all there is to it."

"Ha! You are concealing something, Tiaa." Meret picked up an overripe fig, then put it down and wiped her fingers on her gown. "I want the truth. You make it your business to know everything. Tell me what was missing, or I'll—I'll tell the captain to turn right around and go back." The whole thing had become a matter of principle by now. Meret was determined to assert her authority, even though she hardly thought a missing jar or serving plate was worth such a fuss, even from the workshop of the famous sculptor Smendes. So long as the statue of Taweret was safely on board—

And suddenly she caught her breath. *Was* the statue of Taweret on board? In all the hullabaloo at the wharf, she had not actually seen the statue. Surely it would have been carried onto the boat with some ceremony, wouldn't it? But there'd been so much going on, she hadn't even thought of the statue. Oh, how could she have forgotten about it?

"Tiaa!" she said with a sense of foreboding. "The statue of Taweret—is it on board? Did you see it?"

At this, Tiaa's composure cracked. She twitched in her seat, put bony fingers nervously to her face, then clenched her hands. But no longer could she put it off. With a heavy sigh, she spoke.

"The statue of the goddess, dear Princess—the statue is . . . missing. I made all possible inquiries but could learn nothing more. It is . . ."—Tiaa gave a helpless shrug —"simply not here."

Gazing keenly at her old nurse, Meret knew she was hearing the truth. She turned aside to think over this strange turn of events. So Taweret was missing—Taweret would not be with her. What could this mean? Had the great Smendes failed in his special commission? Or might the statue have been stolen? But who could possibly steal such a precious object? No common thief could get away with it.

Meret remembered her father's words: *Taweret will be with you.* She knew those words meant far more than the comforting effect of religion. Taweret was to be the visible reminder of her father's support, the king's presence. The statue would serve not only to confirm her new role, but to assert Pharaoh's supreme authority over the Sacred City itself. And now it appeared that the goddess would *not* be with her.

She felt Tiaa's cold hand laid gently on hers. "Don't worry, Princess. There must be an explanation. The statue will be found and brought to you soon, I'm sure."

Meret glanced at the nurse in faint appreciation but didn't believe a word of it. Under the warm sun of afternoon, she felt a chill of fear.

Aside from the one missing object, the trip went smoothly. Meret had no complaint about the royal barge that was carrying her to the Sacred City. With its fragrant cedarwood colorfully painted and softened by drapes of crimson silk, it was almost as elegant as her chambers at the palace. Every day she was stuffed with delectable food—roast beef and goose, rare fruits brought from distant shores, honey and sweet cakes in fanciful shapes, even bread with no grit in it.

But there was absolutely nothing Meret could *do* except lounge upon her cushions. Every time she made a move to do something for herself, someone quickly did it for her. As for a pleasant hour reading an ancient text now and then— no possibility of that. She had to be on display every minute. And if she let her thoughts drift into the realm of what might have been, Tiaa would quickly snap her out of the wistful mood.

"Get that gloom off your face, Princess. At least look serene."

The golden fleet stopped at every town along the river. At each port the entire population was waiting along the riverbank to greet the princess with happy smiles and thunderous cheers, whooping and shouting, singing and clapping, banging tambourines and waving flags. Jugglers tossed knives; acrobats did backflips. No doubt about it, all of Egypt was thrilled.

At the same time, Meret felt quite sure that the celebration had not been left entirely to chance. Her father's agents had made certain that the royal procession would be seen everywhere as proof of Egypt's happiness under Pharaoh's rule.

The smile artfully painted on her face grew more fixed with each passing day. Moreover, crammed full of rich food as she was, Meret feared she'd soon look like a plucked goose herself. Often she imagined herself jumping off the golden vessel and running through the streets, across the fields, and out into the sandy wastes, with a defiant cry of freedom.

But there was no escape.

Oh, *why* couldn't she have had a sister who would have been the Divine Wife? Every time Meret let such a thought sneak into her heart, however, she felt ashamed. She would have loved a sister and would not have wished such an unnatural fate for her.

Sometimes Meret turned for silent comfort to her hairdresser, Aset. She had not forgotten Aset's concern for her happiness, and it consoled her a little that at least one person might be thinking of what would be good for Meret—rather than only for Egypt's power and glory.

More often, however, Meret had to sit with Tiaa. She suspected it was partly so she would not be tempted, in her fretfulness, to say or do something outrageous. But at least she could talk freely to her old nurse.

"All this fuss, Tiaa," she said, "and nobody really cares about me. They don't know anything about who I really am or how I feel. They all just assume I'm happy as a cat on a fishing boat."

"As well you should be, my princess," said Tiaa primly, her hands idly playing with a fan of papyrus and silk. She seemed restive, too, but she would never have admitted it. Then she softened. "It's hard, I know, for a young person to sit still for such a long time. You are doing very well. When we get to the Sacred City, everything will be beautiful for you. It will be worth the long journey a hundred times over. You'll see."

Yes, she would soon see about *that*, thought Meret. It would be luxurious living, no doubt, but she had little hope of any more demanding duty than simply to *look* her role. No one in that priest-run city would care what she thought. And although she had tried earnestly not to, she couldn't help recalling the many times her father had talked seriously with her about his business of running the country. Now it seemed as though his respect for her good mind had been almost a cruel joke.

The days passed, sixteen or more. Meret lost count. And then, one morning at long, long last, she heard cries relayed from the first boat in the convoy. The Sacred City was just ahead—the obelisks of the Temple of Amun were already in view! Soon, around a bend in the river, the full magnificence of the city began to display itself. Meret watched with growing awe. Oh, this was indeed a splendid place! She had always thought that her own home city of Saïs must be the finest royal capital in the world, but now she realized it was little more than a dusty provincial town, compared with the Sacred City.

The sight caused a flutter of hope in her heart. If the city was as grand as it appeared, possibly her life here might not be too bad. . . .

Off in the distance, Meret could see more of the Temple of Amun. Its immense pylons reared toward the heavens, behind rows of high poles topped by fluttering banners in scarlet and gold. She had heard of the double column of ram-headed sphinxes leading up to the entrance, and the seemingly endless avenue of much larger sphinxes that led from the Temple of Amun to the Temple of Mut, a good distance away. In spite of herself, Meret felt eager to see the many shrines and obelisks of the two temples, especially Amun's legendary hall of immense columns — as numerous and mighty, it was said, as the great cedars of the Lebanon.

But of course she wasn't allowed to jump up to watch as the royal barge passed that fascinating river front. No, she had to remain stuck in her cushions, idle and dignified.

At last the convoy veered toward the riverbank. As soon as Meret felt the craft secured, she dashed toward the side of the boat. Let them try to stop her! Just once she would get a good look, before being carried off in a grand procession. And in the general excitement, no one did try to stop her. Eagerly she leaned out over the side to see as much as possible.

The whole length of the dock was lined with armed soldiers at attention — not to mention armies of priests. But where were the people, the common people? Although the wharf was garlanded with flowers, there were no musicians, no dancing girls, no ordinary people jumping up and down, singing and shouting. What sort of a welcome was this? The celebration here at the Sacred City should have outdone those of all the other Egyptian towns put together — but there was nothing! Only the solemn priests and the wall of soldiers.

Again her father's voice seemed to echo in Meret's mind — *Taweret will be with you*. Again she felt a chill of apprehension, because the statue was *not* with her.

Meret looked around, wanting to ask what Tiaa thought of it all. But there was no chance. Her attendants fell in line and accompanied her down the petal-strewn bridge set up between boat and shore. Meret saw the priests come toward her—and then everything happened too fast to comprehend. She was suddenly forced backward—she didn't even see who had nudged her—into a palanquin, an elegant litter like the one that had borne her proudly through the streets of Saïs. This one, however, had a framework of curtains surrounding the seat. Scarcely had she sunk into yet more silken cushions than the curtains were drawn, a protective canopy of fine linen dyed a rich purple.

In an instant, Meret was cut off from everything and everyone around her.

CHAPTER 13

For the next two days, Hector did not come or even send any stumbling messengers. Bata had plenty of work at the shop—they had not yet sent him packing, after all. But his heart was preoccupied with the statue. No, not statue, but the goddess Taweret herself! It was a heavy responsibility, having a goddess to look after.

With chagrin, he thought of her hidden in the toolshed under the straw mat and rags that made his bed. Smendes had told him several times about all the work and devotion involved in a deity's daily care, and uneasily he remembered it now.

In the temple, or even in a shrine, the goddess would have squads of priests to take care of her—or her image, which was about the same thing, as Bata understood it. Every morning the priests would wake her, bathe and dress her, feed her, perfume the air around her with incense. When all her needs were met, they would bring her questions and petitions from devoted worshipers. At the end of the day, another group of priests would repeat the routine: feed her a lovely dinner, prepare her for sleep, seclude her so that she could have a good night's rest. The deities, after all, had the same needs as humans, and they had to be cared for accordingly. In that way, Smendes had explained, they would stay healthy and contented, and do their job of running the world properly.

But poor Bata was just one boy, and he had to work from daybreak till early evening at the sculptors' shop. There was no way he could slip off to perform the necessary duties for the goddess. He had to avoid any suspicion, all the while fearing that someone might go into the storage room and discover that the statue was missing.

Each evening Bata explained the situation carefully to the goddess. To his relief and surprise, she made no objection. She seemed to be a very undemanding deity, asking for nothing more than whatever he could provide. In fact, her behavior puzzled Bata. Was this her true nature, or had she some surprise in store for him? Might she be like Hathor the cow-eared goddess, or Sekhmet with the head of a lioness? As everyone knew, those two goddesses loved beauty and goodness—but could fly into a destructive rage on a whim.

Taweret, in contrast, seemed content just to lie down. "It's such a strain, standing up all the time," she said, adding shyly, "in my expectant condition. Just turn me from one side to the other now and then, if you would. The stiffness of my tail makes it uncomfortable to rest on my back. I do wish Smendes had been able to . . . oh, why talk about it." And that, Bata observed, was the closest she came to complaint.

Morning and evening he tried to feed her in as elegant a manner as he could manage. Bread, greens, and boiled eggs were the usual fare, and once even a small piece of fatty mutton. Taweret would take just a little . . . Bata did not presume to watch too closely. He was not altogether certain that she ate anything at all. In any event, when finished, she would kindly allow him to eat the remainder. That, after all, was what went on in the temples, Bata was quite sure. Everyone knew that priests were very well fed indeed.

Bata had no notion of the proper way to address the goddess, and she offered no guidance. He could not call her by her true name, Taweret, like an old friend. Just plain "Goddess" sounded too brusque. At length he decided that the expression "O Goddess" would have to convey his respect.

The boy and the goddess managed to pass two days in this fashion, without anyone noticing anything unusual in the cartwright's toolshed — or the sculptors' storage room. But Bata worried constantly. Would Hector be able to arrange for his part of the journey? Otherwise, Bata had no idea of how to proceed.

After dark on the third day, just as he was about to lie down for the night, a stealthy knock on the rough, ill-hung door of the shed roused him. Peering through a crack, Bata saw Hector and quickly opened the door just wide enough for the Greek to squeeze inside.

"I've been searching half the night for this miserable alley," Hector muttered nervously. Panting, he went on before Bata could say anything. "We're leaving — before dawn! My father agreed; he liked my plan. Things are uneasy in Thebes and he needs to know more. Gave me plenty of money. I'm to stay there a week, then come back."

Bata smiled broadly in relief. "Then everything is set? Did you find a boat that could take us?"

"Two, in fact."

"Two?"

By now Hector had caught his breath. "Just one problem. My father's sending one of his men with me. I told him I could travel alone, but he has to do it his way."

Bata's smile vanished. "You didn't tell him that you already had a — a servant?"

"An Egyptian kid, a worker in a stonecutters' shop? What do you think?"

In his disappointment, Bata flared. "It's not a stonecutters' shop, it's a sculptors' shop! You'd better get that straight."

Hector, surprised at this uncustomary heat from Bata, waved a hand in apology. "Right, I've got it straight. Give me a chance to tell you, for Zeus' sake! I've just come from the docks, talked with another boat captain, and he'll take us. That's why we have to leave at dawn—to give my would-be guard the slip. He'll turn up at the docks for one boat, but we'll already have left on another."

So they could go together, after all. That was a great relief. But they would be followed by a fuming Greek—or maybe a whole battalion, if Hector's guard dared report that General Leander's son had gotten away.

Hector seemed to sense Bata's uneasiness. "Don't worry," he said. "We'll manage all right, and I don't think the fellow will get in much trouble. My father knows I can be just as stubborn as he is. And just as clever at getting out of a trap. So get yourself ready and—" He stopped short. "Do you have the statue?"

As Bata assured Hector that the statue was safe in his possession, a vital question struck him. Would the goddess reveal herself to the Greek? Well, they would find out soon enough.

Hector left after telling Bata how to find the right boat. Bata then gathered together his few garments and tied them in a bundle. Thankful to have the cloak that Hector had given him, he wrapped the goddess carefully in the fine black wool. At last, weary but afraid to sleep, he sat leaning against the crumbly mud-brick wall, dozing off and on.

The night was still pitch-black when Bata roused himself and splashed some water on his face. Hoisting the bundle of clothes on his back, he carefully picked up the well-wrapped goddess, edged out the door, and made his way through the alleys.

With every step, Bata's conscience jabbed. To think of sneaking away from the workshop without even a word! Now he would surely lose his job. But he was even more sure that he was doing the right thing—and that Smendes would have wanted it that way.

At the docks Bata found the boat without difficulty. The lanky captain, pacing back and forth nervously, snapped at him. "D'you think we've got all night and all day? Step lively, boy! Wait—what've you got there in that bundle?" He stared at the large object in Bata's arms.

"It's—it's just my master's things," Bata stammered. "His clothes and sandals, his—his armor and—"

Luckily, at that moment Hector sauntered up. "What do you expect?" he said to the captain coolly but with an engaging smile. "I'm not going to carry everything myself, when I've a strong lad to help me. Come on, Bata, we've got a good corner on the forward deck."

Bata found some packs and bundles already in the small area that Hector had claimed. No sooner had Bata put everything under a makeshift awning than the captain gave orders to release the mooring ropes. The craft swung out into the river, propelled by a few oarsmen.

Soon the sail filled with the predawn wind. The current of the Nile, flowing from south to north, would be against them for the entire trip. The wind, however, would help, for it almost always blew in the opposite direction, from north to south. Whenever the breeze became too light, the muscles of the boat's crew would keep the vessel going.

Hector gestured toward the cloak-wrapped bundle that contained the goddess. "You'll have to admit, it looks a bit strange," he said in a low voice. "But I guess the captain believed you. He was getting jittery, with good reason. I paid him quite handsomely, you see, and being no fool, he figured I was trying to give someone the slip. Probably afraid the whole Greek army might come after us at the last minute."

In the dawn light, Bata looked around at the boat. It was not, in fact, a very impressive craft. A cargo boat, its deck was laden with sacks of root vegetables and large bales of flax. Three young cattle were tied in the rear section. The whiffs that came from their direction were only partially off-set by a much pleasanter fragrance — a stack of freshly sawn cedar planks from the mountains of the Lebanon. Undoubtedly the boat that Hector was supposed to take would have been more worthy of the Greek commander's son. A young man seeking adventure, however, couldn't be too choosy.

Besides Bata and Hector, there were only four paying passengers. Three appeared to be small merchants or crafts-men, while the fourth, who glanced about him with a pained and superior air, looked like a scribe. The passengers simply settled with their belongings on the deck, wherever they could. One crew member kept a pot of beans stewing on a little clay stove. That would provide meals for both crew and passengers, along with fresh provisions from the riverside villages at which the boat would stop.

There was no special place on board to wash or tend to any other personal needs. But there was a very large river close by, which was all anyone really needed.

The glowing sun rose above the flat fields to the east, sending long shadows from the farmers already at work. As the hours passed, the sun god Ra followed his course high overhead. Bata, seeing no boat that appeared to be chasing them, soon allowed the easy rhythms of the vessel, the warm sun, and the fatigue from his restless night to lull him into a long nap. Just before he dropped off, the boat's resident cat, a rangy, half-wild gray beast, curled up beside him and the bundle containing Taweret. Bata wondered whether the animal, closer than humans to the divine realm of nature, somehow sensed the presence of a deity.

When Bata awoke, he drowsily watched the banks of the Nile with their bright green fields, rich dark earth, and groves of date palms. But he soon grew restless. Since childhood, he had passed few days that were not filled with work, even on the many festivals and holidays, and he was not used to feeling lazy. He was glad to have a goddess to attend to. In spite of the difficulties, he felt happily aware that for the first time in his life he was taking care of somebody. He had somebody whose well-being depended on him . . . as he had depended on old Smendes.

Every morning Bata served Taweret her beans and onions, and every evening he presented whatever delicacy he and Hector had been able to buy along the way. But he could do little else. No bathing or dressing or waving of incense pots. Even the serving of meals had to be carried out as stealthily as possible. Fearing that someone on the craft might get curious, Bata persuaded Hector that one of them must remain with their belongings at all times. Not surprisingly, it was Bata who kept watch most of the time. Hector missed no chance to go ashore and explore any ancient temples or crumbling palaces worth seeing.

At the same time, Hector was clearly on edge. Bata often caught him brooding, a pensive sadness alternating with nervous frowns. Was he thinking of the princess Meret and his foolish, hopeless love for her? Possibly, thought Bata, Hector was not so confident of saving the princess from the god's household as he pretended to be. And maybe it was the Greek's own feelings of frustration that made him criticize

Bata for coddling what he thought of as simply a piece of carved stone.

"Look," said Hector. "You don't have to go through all that nonsense of feeding and tending . . . *her*. I know the priests are supposed to do that sort of stuff in the temple, but not you, Bata. Look, it's just a statue, it's not alive. Be rational, for Zeus' sake!"

When he could do so privately, Bata apologized to the goddess for his companion's attitude. He asked whether he should try to make Hector believe in her reality, but Taweret advised him otherwise.

"Let him be," she said. "Either he believes, or he does not believe. Faith rises from deep hidden wells, and there's little you can do . . . except by your own example."

Late one evening when they had been on the river for about five days, Hector seemed unusually thoughtful. The other passengers and most of the crew had already settled down for the night, and Bata sensed that Hector wished to talk.

"There's something," Hector muttered hesitantly, "I want to say. I should have said it before."

Bata waited, unable to guess what was coming.

"It's . . . I'm sorry about your master . . . whatever his name was."

Bata's throat tightened. "Smendes."

"Smendes. I had other things on my mind when you told me. It wasn't right of me. . . . I'm sorry. He was a good sculptor."

"He was a good master," said Bata quietly. "And a good man. He will soon be with Osiris in the Heavenly Fields." This, then, was the Greek's expression of sympathy, and Bata accepted it.

Hector had not finished, however. "I know you Egyptians believe your gods help you in the afterlife," he went on. "What about this one, the statue, Taweret? Do you think she will help Smendes? Is that part of her job?"

"You don't know about Taweret? Then I'll tell you about her," Bata said. "She will be with Smendes, certainly, for she is a loving protector. But her usual job is to care for the most helpless, women and children. She helps mothers bring their babies safely into this world so that they may grow up to lead good lives."

"Oh." Hector was quiet for a moment. The midnight silence was broken only by the dark waters lapping at the sides of the boat, the gentle huffing of the canvas overhead, and snores from other corners of the deck. When Hector spoke again, even though in a whisper, there was a rough edge to his voice. "Did she bless your mother, Bata?"

"I don't know," answered Bata softly. "I never knew my mother. I never even knew what happened to her. All I can hope is that she did not suffer too much in life."

Another long moment passed. "I remember my mother," said Hector at last. "I knew her for nearly nine years, and I loved her more than anything in the world. For years she tried to bring me a brother or sister. Then finally she did, a little girl. But they both died within a day. No deity in the world could have saved them . . . only knowledge and skill that no one had. I remember how my father raged and cursed the gods. He vowed to leave the islands—and their gods—forever. That's why we have wandered ever since, he and I."

Later, when Hector was asleep, Bata heard the goddess stirring. He told her what the Greek had said, and she sighed deeply.

"Yes, I know. I know about every mother and every new child. But I can help only if I'm wanted. That is my joy, and my sorrow."

Gently, Bata tucked the wool cloak around Taweret. In the light of the stars and a flickering oil lamp attached to the mast, he could see that she was indeed grieving.

CHAPTER 14

Inside her curtained palanquin Meret could see nothing, nor could she be seen. With a sudden lurch that sent her grabbing for something firm, the seat was lifted, and she could feel herself being borne away. Up some steps the litter rose, and then it moved along a level route.

She could hear men shouting at people to get out of the way. She could hear women singing, sistrum rattles shaking, priests chanting. But what she did not hear was any sound of jubilation. Even the singing and sistrum shaking had a solemn sound to it, almost funereal. Why? What could this possibly mean? Once she caught her breath, Meret's surprise turned to disappointment and then anger. If she had to be here, at least she should be greeted properly!

But where on earth, the princess wondered as she rocked along, was she being taken? To the Temple of Amun, or somewhere else? The great temple had appeared to be quite close—surely they should have reached it by now. Light filtering through the purple canopy tinged her white linen dress a lovely lavender—and her skin a deathlike hue.

An unpleasant thought struck her: it's as if only the outside of the future Divine Wife matters, while the girl inside dies.

The little flutter of hope she had felt on first viewing the Sacred City was by now feeble indeed. Where were Tiaa and Aset, or any of those servants and attendants and musicians from her journey? So tiresome then—but how glad Meret would have been to see a familiar face now! Her stomach felt queasy, and she wondered how soon she might have a chance to use a commode.

On and on marched the palanquin carriers. The accompaniment of singing and chanting grew weaker, as though the priests and temple women were getting tired and dropping out. Well, let them. All Meret wanted right now was to be let down to solid earth and allowed a moment in private.

Suddenly tipped back among her cushions, she felt herself being taken up a long flight of steps. Then the soft purple light vanished, darkness enveloped her, and the air became cool, perfumed with incense. Good, she thought, this must be the palace. Maybe she was being brought to her own quarters first.

The palanquin was set down—what a relief!—and the curtains drawn on one side. Meret found herself in a high-ceilinged hall with slim lotus-topped pillars. Straining to see in the dimness, she looked around for a familiar face. No one. A row of female attendants stood silently in straight blue dresses, all alike. Their faces were expressionless. One of the women stepped forward and impassively offered Meret a hand as she struggled to get up from the seat. The litter carriers had all vanished as soon as the chair was set down. So far as Meret could see, there were no male officials or servants present.

Now the attendant led her to a large older woman who had mysteriously appeared in the midst of the blue gowns. This personage stood stiffly erect in a stark white sheath, a heavy gold pectoral resting upon her ample chest. In the dim light, her broad face gave the impression of a royal statue, slightly weathered, and her wig was so large that only her impressive solidity, Meret thought, must keep her in balance. Could this be the Divine Wife, the revered Khnumut, herself?

The woman spoke in a high, flat voice. "Welcome, Princess Meret. We have anticipated your arrival for many days. The Divine Wife hopes your journey proceeded in all comfort and order. You will be shown to your private chambers now, that you may rest and be refreshed. Tomorrow, in full ceremony, you will be presented to the Divine Consort of Amun."

So this forbidding lady was just a sort of dignitary. An underling, really. That gave Meret some confidence. She bowed slightly and started to say a few words of polite response. To her surprise, she was promptly hushed by a small but unmistakable gesture from the woman. What, would she not be allowed to speak here? Again, she wished for Tiaa's prickly but reliable support.

Then Meret was led out of the hall. In the dark corridors, she got only fleeting impressions of her surroundings. Exquisitely painted walls rose on either side of her, and little tongues of flame flickered in heavy brass braziers, as though in futile attempt to lick away the heavy shadows. The row of blue-garbed attendants accompanied Meret and her guide down a hallway, up a short flight of steps, and at last into a spacious suite.

In silence, the chief attendant showed Meret through the rooms. There was a comfortable bed on four golden lion feet and, yes, in a corner behind a screen, an elegant commode of carved wood with a basin of water on a table nearby. Now if they would just leave her alone for a while, she would soon feel ready to face whatever lay ahead.

• • •

The sun had set before an evening meal was served to the princess. She had watched the lingering rays fall through a chink in the heavy drapes that covered the one window in the sitting room. Why were the curtains drawn everywhere? Why was the palace kept so dark, as if the light and air of the outside world were somehow dangerous? She was tempted to yank back the drapes, but decided it best not to assert her own will too soon. Surely, tomorrow she would be taken around the palace grounds and shown the gardens and pools, the birds and flowers and pet animals. She would see Tiaa. Everything would be much nicer tomorrow.

Three attendants eventually appeared bearing covered bowls made of delicate ceramic. Meret watched with concealed eagerness as they set a small round table, big enough for only one person, and placed the bowls on a crisp linen covering. Motioning to Meret to seat herself, they then lifted the covers, revealing a savory cut of meat cooked with vegetables, a piece of fine bread, and a small cake. One of the women poured wine into a beaker of purple glass.

"Royal Princess, do you wish anything more?" she asked as Meret unfolded a napkin trimmed with gold thread. Aside from the brief greeting by the woman in white, those were the first words anyone had spoken to Meret since she had disembarked from the royal barge. She looked up, trying to read the woman's expressionless face.

"No, you may go," said Meret, keeping her voice cool and firm. "I shall ring the little bell when I'm finished."

The women left with measured steps, and as soon as the door swung shut, Meret fell upon her food as though she had not eaten in days. The wine was especially comforting, different from the wines of the north, with a trace of some unusual herb. A nice meal—at least they had good cooks at this palace. Meret's spirits rose a notch. A little later the attendants returned to remove the dishes and lay out a nightdress, as delicate as flower petals.

But enough of this silent coming and going! Meret was beginning to feel sleepy. "I wish to be by myself," she announced. "I see that everything I need is at hand. You may leave now."

The attendants glanced questioningly at one another. For a moment Meret was afraid they would not obey her wishes. But then they bowed and left, closing the door silently.

Tomorrow will be much better, said Meret to herself as she removed the band of golden flowers that encircled her wig, and then the hated wig itself. The attendants, she thought, were stiff because they didn't know anything about her. Maybe they were just as nervous as she was. Tomorrow, after her presentation to the Divine Wife, everything would be more pleasant. Then people would feel free to talk to her.

Meret yawned. So tired . . . it had been a long, strange day. But she had to get out of her tightfitting dress . . . tighter than ever now, thanks to all the cakes and roast goose she had eaten on her journey. Maybe she should have asked for some help. Oh, never mind, she could manage.

Dropping the dress over a small wooden chair, Meret gratefully slipped on the filmy nightgown. Having carefully removed the green powder from her eyelids, the black kohl from her brows and lashes, and the rouge from her lips, she picked up a large hand mirror of highly polished silver and, with heavy-lidded eyes, studied her reflection. Was she pretty, without all the embellishment? If she had not been forced to marry a god, would she, as Aset had wished, have become a beautiful and beloved wife someday?

As she gazed into the mirror, her eye caught the reflection of a slight movement behind her. What was there in the room that could move? Oh, the door, of course. The door appeared to be opening . . . silently.

For a moment Meret stiffened with fear. Then she told herself to relax; it was just one of the attendants checking to see if anything was needed. She lowered the mirror, placed it with deliberation on the ivory-inlaid table, and turned around.

There stood a woman whom Meret had not yet encountered. A small, severe wig came low on her brow, above a thin face sculpted by age. Her only ornament was a single pendant of intricately designed lapis and jade, resting on a gown that shimmered as though woven of gold. Past middle age, she stood with a slightly hunched posture and protruding abdomen, her head tilted back. Silently she appraised Meret. No light could be seen in her eyes, deep-set in heavily darkened lids.

Meret knew, without a trace of doubt, that she was now in the presence of the Divine Wife herself. But why at this hour? Why with no ceremony? Well, it would surely be explained . . . and Meret must behave in the proper way, no matter how surprised . . . and sleepy. She stepped forward and bowed as deeply as she could, her head nearly touching her knee.

When she raised her head, she saw that the Divine Wife was not alone. On either side of her stood an attendant in an unadorned, straight blue dress. Unlike the others, however, these were Kushites from the south, extraordinarily tall women. Meret had seen men of this remarkable race, tall as palms and dark as ebony, with the strength and beauty of black cheetahs. Yet she couldn't help a gasp of astonishment at the sight of these giant women. Only the whites of their eyes marked their features in the heavy shadows.

The Divine Wife spoke. "So . . . the princess Meret has arrived, the young royal princess sent by our exalted Pharaoh. And a beautiful princess she is, indeed." Unbending slightly, she continued in a more conversational tone, her voice low and husky but with a curious sweetness. "Have you anticipated with great joy, my princess, the honors and powers that await you?"

Blinking, Meret tried to gather her wits enough to remember the correct phrases. "It is honor enough, O Divine Wife, to be in thy presence, prosperity and long life to thee. Princess Meret can ask for nothing more."

A smile twisted the woman's thin lips. "A graceful response." She lifted a hand slightly. In a few strides, the two Kushite attendants covered the distance from the door to the spot where Meret stood. They positioned themselves at her elbows, one on either side. The startled girl could hear their breathing and, for just an instant, could not help glancing up at one of them in amazement. Returning her gaze to the Divine Wife, she found it held hypnotically.

"The princess is not only beautiful, but wise," continued the Divine Wife. "How fortunate that she demands so little."

An instant later Meret could see nothing. Had she at last fallen asleep, dropping from fatigue? No, she was awake, she knew it. Something black had suddenly enveloped her—and now she was aware of an ironlike grip on each of her arms.

The strange husky voice was speaking again. With her last trace of will, Meret strained to hear.

"No harm need come to you, Princess Meret, if you cause no trouble. But I doubt that you will ever see your home again—and you will *never* see the Sacred City again. Pharaoh will learn soon enough that his plan has brought him no gain, and only grievous loss. He will learn that the Sacred City is not his to command. It is *mine*—and so it shall remain."

Mine . . . the wine . . . The words echoed for a second in Meret's head, and then she lost all consciousness.

CHAPTER 15

Bata and Hector watched wonderstruck as their boat sailed past the great temples. Pylons, flags, and immense statues of long-dead kings reared majestically to the skies. The golden tips of obelisks reflected dazzling rays intermittently as the midafternoon sun moved in and out of the clouds.

But Bata was feeling some qualms. Now that they had actually reached the Sacred City, the whole venture did not look anywhere near so simple as it had at the start. He had no idea, not the slightest notion, how to find the princess. Even if he managed to get to the right palace, would he be allowed to march in and present the statue himself? Not very likely.

As he considered the suddenly overwhelming challenge ahead of him, Bata became aware of something strange right before his eyes. Here they were, sailing past the massive temple docks—and there was no sign of the royal fleet from Saïs. A number of luxurious craft were moored at the riverside, but nothing with royal insignia.

He turned to Hector. "Where are the barges and boats that brought the princess? Could we have gotten here before them?"

Hector, too, looked puzzled. "Hardly. We couldn't possibly have passed them on the river without noticing. I don't know . . ."

Finally the boat reached a poor part of town. Here the river front was a jumble of rickety wharves and vessels for heavy transport. Porters and vendors filled the air with their shouts and shrill cries.

As soon as the boat was secured, Hector grabbed his pack and ran down the gangplank, followed by Bata with most of the bundles and Taweret well wrapped in the cloak. Bata hustled to keep up as Hector charged through the crowds on the docks. Bursting with nervous energy, the Greek was ready to push people around.

"First of all, I want to find a decent place to stay," he tossed back over his shoulder. "Have a good bath and look like a civilized man again. Leave our stuff."

Bata agreed, knowing he would have to carry the goddess everywhere they went, keeping her well concealed. Yet surprisingly, she seemed quite easy to lift now. Her body felt solid and bulky, but not hard or heavy.

Taweret seemed to read his thoughts. Her voice came to him softly through the cloak. "You will not have to carry me forever, young Bata. Before long I expect to relieve you of the burden."

"Oh, it is no burden—"

"Of course I'm a burden," she answered a bit testily. "But I shall soon be able to take better care of myself. You will see."

The two boys elbowed their way along, trying to get an idea of their surroundings and look for a likely inn. Now and then someone better dressed than the typical rabble, a merchant or minor official, chided them. "Watch it there! Who do you think you are?" But with a second look at Hector's light skin and Greek tunic, the person would quickly back off. Was this a sign of respect for the foreigners — or distaste? Bata wasn't sure.

When they had made their way out of the waterfront area, Bata and Hector found themselves in a large open square with palms and gardens at one end. Here the people were well dressed and prosperous looking. A cluster of market women sat at the near side of the square. On the other side stood a row of well-made houses, two or three stories high with handsome facades and windows cut in decorative shapes.

But Bata sensed something subdued about the atmosphere and soon noticed the reason why. At several spots around the square, soldiers stood at attention, in small groups but fully armed. And not just Egyptian, but Greek soldiers. Although somewhat more casual in their posture, the Greeks appeared to be observing the scene attentively.

When Hector caught sight of them, he frowned. "Makes me nervous, the way they're just looking around at everybody. Wonder if they've gotten word about my coming without my escort. Well, I'll go see the commander, of course, but not right away."

"Take care," said Bata. "There's a bunch of them — don't turn — over by that pool." The soldiers were looking in their direction. Maybe the Greeks had, in fact, been alerted to watch for Hector's arrival. Or maybe something else was going on.

There was no sign, however, of what *should* have been going on. Where were the welcoming festivities for the future Divine Wife? Nowhere did Bata see any flags, banners, or displays of flowers. There were no crowds of excited people, no sign whatsoever of holiday mood. If the royal fleet had already arrived and departed, and the princess had been taken to her palace, at least there would still be some left-over decoration in the streets. And if the princess had not yet arrived, then the city should be decked out brilliantly to receive her.

Far from celebratory, the atmosphere seemed ominous — and all the more so as a sudden strong gust of wind whipped through the plaza. The sun had now disappeared into a thick cloud bank.

Something else looked odd. Many of the people in the square no longer had the air of casual shoppers. The crowd was starting to drift in one direction. Soon it became a steady stream, more and more purposeful, heading toward a broad street that apparently led from the square to some other part of the city. Where were they going . . . and why? The Egyptian soldiers were growing more edgy, it seemed to Bata, but made no move to interfere.

Meanwhile, the Greek soldiers still appeared to be watching Hector. Catching Hector's eye, Bata jerked his head toward the nearest group of market people. Here they might mingle inconspicuously among the sellers and shoppers until they could figure out what was going on.

Spotting a bright-eyed old woman sitting on a crude stool, with a few skinny geese for sale, Bata decided to chat with her. She looked like the familiar market women he knew in Saïs, full of local gossip.

"Greetings, old mother," he said. "We need a place to lay our heads. Do you know an inn where the fleas aren't too fierce?"

She grinned, the toothless mouth in her leathery brown face yawning like a well in a barren field. "Just come, eh? Just in time for the goin's-on!"

"Goings-on?" echoed Bata innocently. "Why, what's going on?"

"Didn't you hear? The princess, of course, the young princess!"

Hector grabbed Bata by the elbow. "Did she say something about the princess? Ask her — has the princess arrived?"

But before Bata could speak again, the old woman pointed a shaky finger toward the crowd. "Look! Everybody's goin' to the palace square—you better hurry, get yourselfs a place. I'd be there, too, if me legs would hold me better—and me birds didn't hold me back!" She let out such a cackle of mad laughter that the geese were startled and added their own feeble honking. Another gust of wind tore through the marketplace, as though nature, too, were enjoying a malicious laugh, and the old woman struggled to hold on to her head-cloth.

Bata turned to Hector. "She says everybody's going to the palace square—something big is going on."

"Good!" Hector's face lit up. "They must be having a ceremony to welcome the princess. Let's go!"

With a nod at the old woman, who thrust one of her squawking geese at them in a late effort to make a sale, Bata and Hector hurried away and joined the crowd. The sky was growing darker with every minute, reinforcing the feeling of urgency.

Soon they found themselves in another open square, grand in size and apparently the very center of the Sacred City. On the far side rose the broad steps and magnificent facade of a huge palace, with other edifices almost equally grandiose flanking it. Bata gazed around him, awe-struck. The royal palace at Saïs was modest compared with this.

Already the square was seething with excited crowds. People of every description seemed to be eagerly awaiting something. There were beggars in rags, nobles in fine robes, and every sort of person in between . . . Egyptians, Kushites, Asians, Libyans, Syrians, Canaanites, Phoenicians, Hebrews, all in their distinctive styles of dress. Here the military presence was unmistakable. Egyptian soldiers, hands on weapons, were stationed on the palace steps and throughout the crowd. Thus far they were merely watching—but they looked ready to crack a few heads, if need be.

Above the hubbub, Bata gradually became aware of one strong voice. Where the crowd was thickest a platform had been set up, packed with military officers and priests. One, who seemed to be a priest blessed with high rank and a thunderous voice, was starting to speak. The crowd quieted down. As the two boys made their way closer, Bata began to catch the words.

". . . Does Egypt, the First Land, tremble when even the mightiest of enemies threatens?"

The crowd roared, "NO!"

"Can Egyptians, the First People, accept this craven insult?"

"NoooOOO!" A fierce gust of wind seemed to magnify the sound into a howl.

Hector, tight-faced, pulled at Bata's arm. "What is it? What's he saying?"

Bata could only throw him a baffled, scared look. This was no welcoming ceremony—this was an angry, dangerous mob.

The priest went on with his mounting harangue. "In all the history of the First Land, since the beginning of time, has Egypt ever suffered such an outrage?"

"Nooo . . ." This time the crowd sounded a little less sure—after all, Egypt's history was longer than anyone knew. But soon they came back with a good bellow. "NOOOO!"

"Then what must Egypt do to avenge this monstrous insult?"

The crowd responded exactly as it was meant to. "Fight . . . *Fight* . . . FIGHT! War . . . *War* . . . WAR!!!"

As though the heavens had heard and answered, heavy gray clouds rolled over the square. Large drops began to fall like missiles from an army of slingers. Before the frenzied crowd knew what was happening, a deluge was upon them.

CHAPTER 16

Meret rocked lazily with the rhythm of the boat. She'd been on the boat just about forever, it seemed. Yet now it was rocking harder . . . maybe they were going over the fearsome cataracts she'd heard of, where the water rushed among huge boulders. That would be interesting. . . . But her pillows weren't soft and comfy at all. They were hard, and they smelled bad. She would demand new ones.

People were talking near her. Strange . . . they didn't sound like Tiaa, or any other of her maids and attendants. Gruff voices, coarse.

Gradually, she became aware of the golden light pouring over her. It must be morning now . . . but she didn't want to open her eyes yet. She would just lie still, until she felt good and ready to wake up.

The voices came nearer. Mumbles took shape as words. Without moving or opening her eyes, Meret began to hear, to listen, and to understand.

"Look at the girl, dead to the world. Easier for us if the stuff they gave her 'ad knocked her off for good."

"Easier, sure, but they're paying us to do a job. No girl, no pay."

"Right, don't remind me. So here we sit in this cursed place, just watching her, damn our luck."

Meret began to grow interested. Who was this poor girl they were talking about? What was the problem? They should tell *her*, Princess Meret, daughter of Pharaoh, and she would set things right.

She opened her eyes. *Where was she?* Propping herself up on one elbow, Meret raised her other hand to shield her eyes.

White. Blinding, unbelievable whiteness, all around her. Massive walls of white rose a little distance away. Was she in an immense temple? But it was so bright — and the walls were broken. Oh, they weren't walls at all — but huge, high rocks! She was outdoors, and above was the sky, an intense, clamoring blue. Then Meret looked down and saw that she was sitting on a ground of pure white sand.

Shading her painfully dazzled eyes, Meret began to search for the voices. Surely they would explain things.

Why, there were two men sitting close by, watching her! That didn't seem proper at all. And where were Tiaa and Aset? Who were these men in long coarse robes? They couldn't be servants in the palace. They looked like . . . desert people, maybe. Sand-dwellers. Well, they had better explain themselves quickly.

Meret tried to sit up straight, the better to confront the men. But she felt strangely weak. "Who are you, and where am I?" she asked, her voice sounding thin and childish.

"And if we don't care to answer?" said one of the men mockingly.

"Why, you must!" said Meret in surprise. "What is this place, and why are we here? I demand to know."

The man gave a short, humorless laugh. He had a belligerent, unshaven jaw — all that could be seen in the shadow of his head covering. "Why, it's a fine place here. Just look around you — see those beautiful white walls? Just like your palace."

"'Cept it's full of evil," broke in the other man. "Nothing lives here, no animal, no plant . . . it's cursed."

"Enough of that, Seneb," warned the first.

"Well, is it cursed?" asked Meret, turning from one to the other. She wasn't particularly alarmed. The whole situation was too bizarre for her to worry about the place being cursed. But confused as she was, she could latch on to only one fact at a time.

The first speaker gave an uneasy shrug. "All right, since you ask, Princess. Yes, the place has a bad reputation around these parts, so that's why we're staying here. Got it?"

Meret shook her head, trying to clear away the muddle. She was surrounded by high white walls, but it was outdoors, and it was an evil place where no one ever came. . . . Why was *she* here? And how long had it been since she was in her room in the — that dark, unfriendly palace, getting ready for bed? And where was that lovely nightdress? She looked down. She was wearing a simple garment of loosely woven, scratchy brown cloth, like the men's robes. Touching her head, she felt only her closely cropped hair. Why, she must look like a boy, a common boy — a desert boy!

No, this was not one bit proper. She was a princess. She must be dressed in fine clothes, and perfumed, and —

Just then the man called Seneb handed her a rough-woven cloth. "Put this on your head, or you'll fry," he said, pointing at the already blazing sun in the east. He appeared to be thinner and more jittery than his companion, his face shadowed by a hood.

"Thank you," said Meret in a dignified way, looking with distaste at the cloth. It wasn't pretty. Already, though, the sun was bothering her, and a light breeze tossed the sand. She struggled to tie the cloth over her head. Suddenly she felt ravenous. "I'm hungry," she said. She couldn't possibly understand anything more until she'd had something to eat. She hoped they had some figs and roast goose.

They didn't. Kai—she'd heard the one called Seneb address him by that name—brought her a hunk of poor bread and a cup of water. The water didn't taste good, but it was wet, and she felt utterly parched.

Blinking, Meret looked around, trying to understand the astonishing place in which she found herself. A short distance away were four horses, the ropes around their necks anchored by large rocks. They didn't look happy at all. Close by, Meret now saw that a rough camp had been set up, a haphazard pile of bags and small rugs spread out on the gleaming white sand. There were several goatskins containing water, or so Meret supposed, having never seen a waterskin before. She wanted some water to wash in. She badly needed a nice bath.

The bread gave Meret energy to make another demand. "I must know how long we're going to be here. I have things to attend to. I have obligations." She couldn't quite remember what those obligations were . . . but surely she should be doing something.

Kai guffawed. "Now isn't that interesting! Things to attend to! Such as . . . ?"

Meret tried hard to think. He wanted to know about her obligations . . . so she must tell him. Oh, if only she had listened more closely when Tiaa was lecturing about her duties as the— Oh! Tiaa! Where was she? And Aset, and every one of her servants? *They* were her responsibility, now that she was so important, and she must look after them.

Drawing a deep breath, Meret spoke. "I arrived in . . . in the Sacred City with many attendants, servants, officials,

and—and others. Not to mention things I would need and . . .
other things. Lots of everything, and people. I must be
informed as to the whereabouts of all my . . . people from
the royal city of Saïs. Where are they?"

"Oh, you'd like to know, would you?" said Kai with a
short laugh. The one called Seneb, sitting hunched by himself, snickered.

A spark of anger flared in Meret's still-muddled mind.
"Yes, tell me! Where is Tiaa? She will be furious if anything
bad happens to me. And you won't like having Tiaa furious
with you. Not one bit."

Kai did not answer immediately. He got up and joined
Seneb for a moment to confer, then returned and sat in his
former place near Meret. "No harm in telling you, I guess . . .
you're not likely to be seeing your Tiaa anytime soon—or
anyone else."

"But I insist—"

"Princess, you're not in a position to insist on anything.
Listen, because I'm not going to tell you more than once.
Maybe you noticed a certain, shall we say, military presence
when your royal convoy arrived in the Sacred City. Hmm?
So, what do you think they were there for? Right. Soon as
you were safely out of the way, the army took over. Your
people probably hadn't any idea what was happening.
Didn't put up much of a fight, anyway, from what I hear."

It was coming back to her now, the bewildering
moments of her arrival in the Sacred City. So that was why
she had so quickly been pushed into the covered palanquin
and whisked away. Why, what a traitorous crime—to capture
the royal flotilla!

"But—but—why?" Meret sputtered. "They had no
right—Where—?"

"Calm yourself, Princess. The boats've all been taken up
the river where they'll be out of the way. If the folks on 'em

have any sense and make no trouble, they won't be hurt."

With this report, the fuzziness in Meret's mind grew into grim realization. She sat subdued for a moment, then thought again of her royal duty. She would make one more attempt.

"You said they are not being mistreated —"

"If they make no trouble."

"Do — do they have enough to eat?"

Kai gave another humorless laugh. "Better worry about yourself, Princess."

The sun was getting hotter by the minute. Looking around her, Meret saw that here and there an isolated pillar rose from the desert floor, eroded by eons of wind. The only shade was at the foot of one of these towerlike white rocks a short distance away. She moved over to sit there, and after a few minutes' silence she felt ready to launch another question.

"It's only fair for me to know who you are. You're not sand-dwellers, even though you're dressed that way."

"In the desert, you dress for the desert. Look, Princess." Kai pulled down the loose neck opening of his robe enough to reveal a better fabric and the glint of metal. "Does that give you a clue?"

A military uniform, thought Meret. From the traitorous army that seized my royal fleet. Or maybe guards from the palace. "I see," she said. "Then the least you can do is tell me why we're here. And for how long."

Kai got up and went over to the pile of baggage dumped on the sand. He returned chewing a piece of dried meat and handed one to Meret. It looked to her as though he was deliberately taking his time in answering. When he sat down again, he said, "All right, I've probably told you too much already — might as well tell you a little more. Well, the plan was to stay only one night in this cursed place. It's not the kind of hiding place I'd choose. I don't like evil spirits any more'n the next man. Although I'm not so . . ." Meret saw him turn his head slightly in the direction of his companion.

"Watch it, Kai," muttered Seneb.

Disregarding, Kai went on. "But now it looks like we'll be here a little longer, on account of the trail's been washed out and we'll have to find a different one. Nothing ever works out the way it's supposed to."

"A different trail . . . to where?"

"To where we're taking you."

"And where is that?"

Kai hesitated, then shrugged. "Our orders are to take you as far as the sea. Then somebody else'll take you to the far shore, and that's all we know and all we want to know."

"But . . . ," stammered Meret, "you said we have to stay here awhile. How can we? I mean, how will we have enough to eat and drink?" Tears filled her eyes, and her mouth began to quiver. That made her so angry with herself that she pulled the headcloth over her face. She would *not* let these men see her crying.

She heard Seneb speak. "That's what I'd like to know. What good is *he* doing, anyway? Why doesn't he get going, find that other trail?"

Glancing up, Meret saw Seneb's hooded head turn briefly in the direction of the horses. Now she saw a third man, crouching near the animals and gear, as motionless as one of the loosely tied packs. He looked even more shaggy than her two captors, a real sand-dweller, Meret thought.

As if on cue, the sand-dweller silently got up, mounted one of the horses, and rode off into the glare of the sun. The image of his lonely figure against the brightness stayed in Meret's mind, like that of a large bird flying off to some distant shore, perhaps never to return.

CHAPTER 17

The mob scattered like a spilled bucket of barley. In a few minutes the palace square was empty, and every tavern within running distance was full. Not knowing where to turn for shelter, Bata and Hector hustled up one street and down another until they found themselves back in the docks area. Their bundles, including Taweret in the wool cloak, were by now soaked and twice as heavy.

At last they caught sight of a small building that gave off the unmistakable aroma and din of an overstuffed tavern. There they found refuge, squashed in with many other wet, steamy bodies. The tavern owner was happily pouring out his beer with a liberal hand, and the crowd, apparently having already forgotten the infamous insult that Egypt had suffered, grew jollier with every minute.

Hector raised an eyebrow at Bata. "Looks like a fine place."

Before Bata could answer, a shrill voice rose over the hubbub. "Hi there, young fellas! Didn't I tell ye, there's big goin's-on?"

Bata looked around, and there in the corner, surrounded by her terrified geese, squatted the old woman they had met earlier. A familiar face, even one such as hers, was welcome. Maybe she could tell them a little more about the big goings-on.

"Wan't it somethin'? Ain't you glad you're here?" She peered up at the two boys, delighted.

"Yes, indeed," said Bata, shouting to be heard but trying to appear calm. "What about the princess, old mother? You said something—"

"You ain't heard? Oh, may the gods help us—there's terrible things happenin'!" She let out another cackle of lunatic laughter.

Hector jabbed Bata impatiently with his elbow. "What did she say? I can't understand a word."

"I'll tell you soon as I hear anything that makes sense." Then Bata turned back to the woman. "Tell us, old mother, what are these terrible things?"

She took on a conspiratorial look, beckoning him to approach. "The little princess," she mumbled, "the new one what's just come to be the god's wife . . ."

"Yes? I asked you—what about the princess?" He had to lean uncomfortably close to hear her.

"She's *gone.*"

Bata jerked back in surprise. "*Gone?* But—where?"

"The Persians," cackled the goose seller, obviously enjoying the effect of her news. "Yep, dirty Persians took her. Carried her right off. Oh, they's dirty scum, them Persians, all right. *Spies.*"

By now their conversation had attracted attention, and an interested audience was growing. Hector could barely control himself. "What is it? Tell me!"

As he answered, Bata tried to conceal his dismay and shock. "She says—she says the princess has been stolen! Persian spies carried her off!"

He expected Hector to shoot through the roof. To his surprise, the Greek reacted with scorn. "Oh, come on. A crazy old crone babbling nonsense, and you fall for it? Don't be a fool, Bata."

"No, wait! We better—" But Bata got no further. A scruffy-looking man had joined them, elbowing others aside. He set down a large jug of a juice drink that he'd been selling before the downpour.

The juice seller appeared somewhat less addled than the old woman. Forgetting the customary greetings, Bata turned to him and demanded, "What's this all about? What's happened to the princess?"

"God's truth," said the man. "Word come from the palace. The princess was taken away—'most as soon as she got here. Persian spies, folks say. Everybody's talkin', everybody says this means big trouble." Several other tavern patrons joined in, supporting the man's story.

Hector stepped forward, straining to hear. "Is this true? How? Tell us!"

The man shrugged. "Well, all's I can say is what I hear from other folks. They did it, that's all, them rotten Persian rats. And now the army's getting ready to march, but nobody knows where. Some says they's goin' east, try to catch them spies what took the poor young princess. Some says they'll join Pharaoh's army in the north, maybe march on the Persians from there."

"But *why* did the Persians steal the princess?" begged Bata, as if this man were the fount of information.

The drink seller leaned close, and Bata braced himself against the man's breath. "You want to know what I think? Them Persians, filthy dogs, they want to make Pharaoh attack *them* first so's they can come marchin' right across Egypt, killin' folks and ruinatin' the country, just like they done in Asia."

A rumble rose from the circle of beer-soaked listeners. All were eager to add their views, some with reasoned argument, others with clenched fists.

"We'd better get out of here," Bata muttered to Hector. This was no place for a goddess, or for them, either. He clutched his precious bundle tighter than ever and picked up what he could, leaving the rest to Hector. Then, with scant thanks to the goose woman and the juice seller, they forced their way through the crowd toward the open door.

In the fading light, Hector's face was pale and his eyes looked dazed. "I can't believe it," he muttered. "This is unbelievable. Completely impossible."

Bata agreed. But all they could do right now was get out of the tavern, find someplace quieter to put down their bundles, get a little rest, and think.

A muscular young man who had been circulating through the crowd with a large jug of beer intercepted them at the door. "Lookin' for a spot for the night, gents?" he lisped through two missing front teeth, and grinned broadly.

"Yes, we want a room," said Hector, distraught. "And we can p—" With a well-timed stumble, Bata managed to step on Hector's foot. No need to advertise their purse.

Now the proprietor himself approached them, a man in well-spread middle age with tremulous jowls. "Sure, we can take you in, chaps, but don't expect nothin' fancy. You'll have to share the sleepin' room with some other folks—all good honest types, guaranteed. You won't find nothin' better this side o' the palace, let me tell you. There's a lot of travelers come to the city these days."

Bata's arms ached. He didn't like the looks of either the place or the good honest types, but he desperately wanted to put the bundles down for a while. He had no doubt that the goddess, too, was ready to feel solid earth under her again, having been lugged around all afternoon.

Hector said, "Look, we need a room to ourselves. We'll pay for it."

The tavern keeper and the younger man guffawed. But their laughter did not sound meanspirited to Bata, who had learned early in life to judge whether a laugh was good-natured or malicious. After a short conference, the toothless one reported back.

"There's a storage room where our scullery boy slept, before he run out on us. You won't like it—stinks of rotten onions and it's noisy as all the demons in hell, but you can have it to yourselves. For a bit more than our customary rate."

Bata and Hector could indeed smell the room, which adjoined the kitchen, before they reached it. But if cockroaches weren't counted as company, at least it was private. Hector left to Bata the job of settling in while he went back to the tavern. He looked so upset that Bata worried he might get drunk, cause a scene, or say something unwise.

Dumping his other bundles on the dirt floor, Bata set down Taweret with care. "This seems the best we can find, O Goddess," he said softly, removing the wet cloak from her face.

"Then it will have to do." Taweret's statement was philosophical but her tone was crisp, and Bata caught a sharp look in her eye.

"Only for one night," he hastened to add. "We'll find someplace better tomorrow." He wasn't sure of that. The price Hector had been forced to pay for this room had considerably lightened his purse. If that was what the worst innkeepers could get away with, what would a decent place charge?

Taweret grunted. "I did not come to the Sacred City to be hauled around endlessly and sheltered in a demon hole that reeks of rotten onions. But since everything has gone awry, and since the princess may be in an even less enviable situation, we must now develop a new strategy. Quickly."

Bata, feeling completely stumped as to the next step, looked at her with surprise and admiration. "What do you suggest, O Goddess?" he asked.

"First," she said in a businesslike tone, "we have to get through the night. Then, as early as possible tomorrow morning, I am going to consult my sisters. We have no time to waste."

"Your . . . ," said Bata haltingly. "What do you mean, O Goddess?"

Taweret gave a twitch of impatience. "Very simple, young Bata. You will take me to the Temple of Isis. If anyone knows what's going on here, it will be Isis. She understands you mortals better than you understand yourselves."

Bata gaped at the goddess. To think of seeing Isis herself— queen of the age-old pantheon! "Y-Yes," he stammered. "That sounds like an excellent idea."

"Indeed, it's the only rational course," Taweret answered.

Gradually Bata became aware that the pounding rain had stopped. That, at least, was fortunate, for if the torrent had continued much longer, the crude mud-brick building would have slumped about their ears. Having made Taweret as comfortable as possible, he then returned to the tavern.

Bata found Hector sitting alone in a corner, his face rigid with misery. The crowd was thinning out, and the remaining people appeared to be avoiding the Greek. Bata's heart felt pain for Hector. He sat down close by for a while and touched Hector's hand, but there was little he could say. Then he wheedled from the tavern keeper some coarse bread, oversalted cheese, and a couple of duck legs, and took them back to Taweret for her supper.

• • •

The night in the pungent storage room passed slowly, but daylight finally came and brought new resolve to Hector. As soon as he and Bata had their wits in order again, he took his stand.

"I am not staying here while Princess Meret is a prisoner of the Persians. I am going after her, and I won't rest until I've rescued her."

Taken aback, Bata blinked. Surely, even for the impulsive Hector, that was a rash and hasty decision. It would be much better to wait until Taweret had consulted with the great Isis, who might suggest a more reasonable course of action. Bata was every bit as eager for the princess to be found, so that everything would be in order again and he could discharge his sacred mission; but he had no intention of setting off on a wildly impractical search.

Rather than oppose Hector, however, he said, "How can we rescue her, if we don't know where she is?"

Hector answered as though he had thought everything out. "The Persians must intend to take her out of Egypt as directly as possible. I shall make inquiries about the routes to the sea and then follow at top speed."

"Well," said Bata, "I, meanwhile, shall take the—the statue of the goddess to the Temple of Isis to seek divine guidance."

A snort from Hector. "You superstitious Egyptian—a fine waste of time that will be. As for me, I'll strike up a conversation with any Greek soldiers I run into and find out what I can from them, while you walk around the temple lugging the statue. Then we'll meet and see what we've each learned, I in a practical, rational way and you from your—your divine guidance."

"You're seeking out the Greek army?" said Bata. "I hope you're not walking into the lion's mouth."

"Don't worry. Nobody'll think I'm the son of Leander, looking the way I do now and smelling of rotten onions."

Hector flung open the door of the storage room and strode out, somewhat disheveled but once more crackling with determination.

"O Goddess," said Bata after Hector had left, "what do you think of that?"

"I think we should lose no time in proceeding with our own plans," she answered.

Bata packed up all his bundles again, wrapped Taweret, and left the tavern. Skirting large puddles left by the storm, he headed for the square in front of the palace. Already the town was starting to bustle, but people were too busy repairing rain-damaged walls to notice the tall boy with his awkward baggage. Although the war frenzy of the previous afternoon seemed to have been dampened along with everything else, Bata had no doubt that once the sun had dried things off, the priests and military leaders would again start whipping up the crowd.

Soon, in a maze of residential streets, he became confused. Taweret, however, softly gave him directions to the temple area as he trudged along. "How can you tell, O Goddess?" asked Bata, surprised. "Shouldn't I at least uncover your face so you can see?"

"No, young Bata," she answered without hesitation. "It would hardly do for me to be seen. We are coming close to familiar territory. Don't worry, I know my way around the *sacred* parts of the Sacred City."

Eventually, mud-spattered and perspiring, Bata found himself approaching the Temple of Amun. He caught his breath at the sight of the immense walls covered with sacred scenes, the flags snapping in the morning breeze, and the two long rows of sphinxes leading up to the entrance.

Just then, Taweret asked to be set down. Bata was puzzled. Surely she didn't mean to waddle the rest of the way on her own feet? Why, the mere sight of her would cause a riot!

Nonetheless, he did as he was told, carefully setting the cloak-wrapped bundle upright on the gleaming white stone pavement. After a few jerks and twists, the cloak fell away, revealing . . . nothing.

"Wh-where are you?" stammered Bata.

"I told you," answered a voice beside him, "I would not be a burden to you forever. Now that I am in the vicinity of the sacred temples, I can manage nicely on my own. It would not do to flaunt my presence, so I shall proceed unseen."

"But, O Goddess, I don't under —"

"No, of course you don't. How could you? Simply accept my word for it that I can reveal myself or not, as I wish. And while it has been necessary that you carry me through the less sacred parts of the city, here, close to my sister and brother deities, I am a goddess in full command of her powers. Let us proceed."

As Bata picked up and folded the still-damp cloak, he recalled the goddess's words to him at their very first meeting back in the sculptors' storage room. Maybe this was the sort of thing she had meant. He started to walk as though unspoken directions emanated from the unseen goddess. It dumbfounded him, but he saw no reason to question. With many glances at the resplendent Temple of Amun, a city in itself, he trudged on, following his invisible guide.

Soon he reached another separate temple, and there the goddess indicated that they should stop. This temple was infinitely smaller, like a butterfly beside an elephant. It stood in exquisite simplicity, a jewel of a shrine for the jewel among goddesses. Worshipers clustered outside its walls, seeming content just to be at the home of this deity.

"Wait here," said Taweret's voice, and Bata set down his various bundles. From inside the small sanctuary came the sound of sistrum and tambourine. The priests were performing morning rituals to get the deity's day off to a good start.

Time passed. The sun rose higher, and the remaining rain puddles on the pavement shrank to wet smears. More time passed. While Bata knew very well that time did not exist where deities were concerned, he began to feel worried. He could only hope that Isis was giving Taweret helpful advice.

At long last, words came from the air near him. "We must talk in a more secluded place. Let us move on."

Again Bata followed the unseen presence, until he reached a garden at the edge of the temple precinct. There his guide stopped, and the voice of Taweret took on a new tone.

"Well, a good thing we came! Isis is absolutely beside herself. She is behaving like the queen she is—she can be counted on for that, no matter what—but she is terribly distressed. She hates discord, and she fears that trouble lies ahead. The thought of the little princess being carried off into the night has upset her completely. She was so glad to see me—it gave her the chance to express her true feelings."

Bata, with no idea where to look, asked the air, "Then is it true, O Goddess, that the princess has been stolen?"

"Yes, I fear it is. But . . . this is very strange. Isis says it may not have happened quite as the priests have said. She is not sure. The gods have great knowledge, but sometimes it gets confused by . . . forces on the malevolent side."

Bata's throat felt dry. It frightened him to think of malevolent forces, whatever they might be. "Then . . . who?" he asked. "Where could the princess be? Did the sublime and beloved Isis know that, O Goddess?"

"Now this is another strange thing," said Taweret's voice slowly. "Dear Isis—because she is such a tender mother—says she can see the princess. The princess is in captivity, uncomfortable but not suffering too much. And she is imprisoned by high white walls . . . a strange place with white walls."

"Why, that must be the palace here in the Sacred City," said Bata, feeling a moment of relief. "What else could it be? Smendes told me Pharaoh's palace in Saïs has gleaming white walls, so this one must, too. Maybe the spies have hidden the princess right under everybody's nose. The whole palace must be searched — "

"Calm yourself, young Bata. Isis would know if the princess were in the Sacred City, even as a prisoner. No, this is a place some distance away. Toward the rising sun, she said. Immense, with an awesome aura. Isis could say nothing more about it. She was almost incoherent in her distress, and I had a little trouble understanding her."

Things were getting more baffling every minute. High white walls to the east, immense and awesome. That was all they had to go on?

"I guess," Bata said, "we should go find Hector now. I don't think he'll like the idea of looking for white walls in the desert. He's talking to Greek soldiers about how to follow the Persian spies. He's being rational."

A sound like a snort of mild disgust came from near a clump of lilies. "Oh, that young man! I wish you could tell him to listen to me instead of those Greek know-it-alls. All he'll get from them is nonsense. Furthermore, I am by no means finished with my inquiries."

"Oh? Then where should we go next, O Goddess?" Someplace, Bata hoped fervently, where the information would be more enlightening.

But the voice near the lilies was heavy with foreboding. "To the Temple of Sekhmet."

Again Bata started walking as if pulled by invisible ropes. Back past the great Temple of Amun he trudged. By now crowds were gathering, and legions of priests stood in rows. Bata wondered whether the god himself might soon have something to say about the crisis that Egypt faced, but Taweret would not linger.

He hurried on, catching a glimpse of the large sacred lake beside the temple. Soon he found himself on the processional route with its seemingly endless avenue of ram-headed sphinxes. Surprised to be allowed on this sacred ground, Bata wondered whether the presence of Taweret might somehow be protecting him. But no, many people of both high and low status were following the same route.

The throng halted in front of a relatively small temple. Carved in the stone of its forbidding facade, mighty warrior-pharaohs smote enemies left and right. The mood of the crowd at this temple was nothing like that at the Temple of Isis, for the people appeared to be furious. Their faces, men and women alike, were distorted by passion. Instead of quiet prayers, violent words came from their mouths.

"War . . . *War* . . . WAR!"

Sekhmet the lion-headed was the goddess of war. Her followers had come to demand her support for whatever lay ahead.

"Wait here," the voice of Taweret ordered when Bata reached the edge of the crowd. With a sigh he again set down his bundles. Even with Taweret moving by her own means, he was weary of carrying so much baggage.

The crowd was starting to chant, led by priests at the temple entrance. Bata retreated a few steps, to wait until Taweret made herself known to him again. For quite a while he heard nothing, only the growing madness of the crowd. Taweret seemed to be taking too long. Could she be having trouble in her effort to consult Sekhmet?

Suddenly Bata jumped, startled at hearing the familiar but bodiless voice once more at his side. It sounded decidedly nervous.

"Come, we must move on quickly."

Bata picked up the bundles again and started to trudge away from the temple, along the avenue of sphinxes. Several people gave him hostile stares. The looks seemed to say, Why would anyone come to the Temple of Sekhmet, the center of patriotic fervor, and then *leave?* Highly suspicious behavior.

No one actually accosted Bata, however, and eventually he reached a small, neglected shrine in a quiet alley. There the invisible Taweret stopped.

"*That* was unpleasant, I can tell you!" were her first words. "Sekhmet is in a *state*. Rarely have I seen her so excited. And it doesn't become her one bit—she gets quite coarse, if I may say so. Oh, the horror of it all—it worries me dreadfully!"

For a moment Bata felt he should try to calm down the distressed goddess, assure her that things were going to be all right. But he didn't really think it was true. "Please, O Goddess, what did she tell you?" he asked anxiously.

A heavy sigh, from near a broken marble step, came in reply. "She's so worked up, she hardly made sense. I had to keep begging her just to give me a few straight answers to a few simple questions. But the thought of bloodshed and destruction has utterly gone to her head. And ordinarily— you must believe this—she can be quite sweet. But not now. This is the side of Sekhmet that, frankly, I just hate."

After a deep breath, the voice continued more calmly. "You might tell your Greek friend, if he'll listen, what Sekhmet says. If Egypt attacks the Persians, she says, there will be rivers of blood that will make the Nile look like an irrigation ditch. Sekhmet can't say *whose* blood, and she hardly cares — she is too intoxicated to think straight. But of one thing she is sure, and I believe her completely. There will be terrible slaughter. And . . ."

"And?" Bata prompted timidly.

"*I* know who will suffer. Others may make their plans for war — deities and pharaohs, priests and generals. But innocent people must pay the price, and it's my responsibility to care for *them*."

Yes, Bata thought, remembering stories that Smendes had occasionally told him about Egypt's magnificent conquests. It was ordinary folks — women and children — who paid the price of war. War never did *them* any good.

But one thing was now clear to Bata. Hector was right, however self-deluded in his own hopes. They could not wait for the soldiers to find the princess. With the divine guidance of Isis, they must rescue her themselves — before Egypt responded to the Persians' provocation and took the fatal step of attacking first. From now on, with Taweret's support, they would work together.

"We must look for Hector now," Bata said. "We'll find out what he has learned, and then we must get going. Wherever the royal princess is held captive, we must rescue her and as quickly as possible. Maybe in that way we can help prevent some trouble. Don't you think so, O Goddess?"

"We are of one mind, young Bata," came the voice.

CHAPTER 18

Once more Meret tried to take a proud posture. Clearly, these men had no respect for royalty, but she would play her proper role.

"So we are waiting for the guide to find an alternative route, although we don't know whether such a route even exists. That is stupid. If we go back to the Sacred City, Pharaoh will reward you generously. Much more generously than—"

Rude laughter greeted that offer. "Princess," said Kai, "long before Pharaoh ever learns about it, our throats'd be cut. And yours, too. No, Princess, you're better off getting as far away from that place as you can. And us, too!"

Remembering the Divine Wife's cold eyes, Meret knew Kai was right. She did not want ever again to see that haughty, cruel face or feel the grip of those female warriors' hands. Maybe she *was* better off here. At least her captors would talk to her.

For the moment, at least, Meret decided to make the best of her predicament. Gazing around her, she saw again that the camp was set up near a freestanding rock that rose like a pillar in an immense courtyard. Most astonishing of all was the pure white sand. Right above their camp, it appeared to pour down from the top of the rock wall, like a cascade of water, spreading a short distance at the bottom. Everywhere else, the desert floor was of bare, rough, gray stone, sculpted by the wind into jagged little ridges.

Meret picked up a handful of sand. A good wind would blow it fiercely. She hoped the god of the desert, Min, would not choose to whip up a sandstorm anytime soon. As if in answer to her thoughts, a capricious gust whisked the sand from her hand—and then the air was still again. Intensely, eerily still.

Although the night had been cold, the day soon grew hot. Meret was determined not to complain and give her captors the satisfaction of taunting her for being soft. She would be strong. The daughter of Pharaoh must not weaken. If only there were more water to drink—and it didn't taste like goat!

Occasionally she walked around on the rough gray stone of the desert floor. To the east, the white walls and isolated towers of stone dwindled and gradually disappeared. She squinted in that direction, trying desperately to recall the text she had once read describing the land of Egypt, the desert that lay east of the Nile with a sea beyond. But she could remember little, and what good would it do, since she had no idea where she was? For untold distances there might be nothing but bleak, empty wasteland. Not the slightest chance of escape. She would surely die of thirst and be finished off by wild beasts.

In the meantime, the two men appeared to be growing increasingly anxious. Again she approached Kai, the dominant one, and this time he seemed willing to say more.

"Look, Princess," he muttered irritably. "I don't know why the Great Queen—that's what we call her—wants you out of the way. I just do my job. Anyway, she does, and a wise man don't question orders. We were told to take this route, instead of the most direct to the sea. That's so when the army boys come out to look for you, they won't think to come this way. Seeing as the place is evil and cursed and all." He turned to glance at the huge drift of white sand behind him. " 'Course they aren't *supposed* to find you, y'see, so pretty soon they'll go back to the city. And then we'll move on. If that guide can find us a trail that's not washed out."

"I see," said Meret. She chose her next words carefully and tried to keep her voice steady. "Surely somebody in the Sacred City knows that I have disappeared. Somebody must care — I am Pharaoh's daughter, after all. How is it being explained?"

The man's voice took on a sly tone. "That's the whole thing, Princess. The palace put out that the *Persians* carried you off. The Persians, insulting the great Kingdom of Two Lands, so's to cause big trouble. Oh, she got plans, our Great Queen, all right. I tell you what they say in the barracks — though nobody knows for sure. They say she wants to force Pharaoh to move against the Persians — and get whipped. Pharaoh's army wouldn't have a chance, not even with all them hired foreigners. Well, that's what they say. Me, I don't know. I just do my job." He gave a nervous twitch and lapsed into silence.

What wickedness, thought Meret. The impiety of the whole thing! She had always known that the position of Divine Wife carried political power — but it was still a religious role, one that had guided Egypt for ages. And now the proud Khnumut and her followers had proved false, treacherous, everything evil. How could such terrible hypocrisy have anything to do with true religion?

As Meret sat considering the plot just revealed to her, a breeze sprang up. It spun the sand into little towers — like evil spirits taking form—and then died. Meret, too, feared the wind and the weirdness of their surroundings, although not with the superstitious dread that appeared to be gripping her captors.

The long day passed. Ra, in his fiery disk, completed his circuit of the heavens, and the gentle goddess Nut brought the night with its myriads of bright stars. But the desert guide did not return.

Finally Meret lay down to sleep. The white sand, although it could be pummeled into humps and hollows, was as hard as rock under her thin blanket. Before she dropped off, again she heard voices and had the sensation of starting the dreadful day all over again. This time the words slithered toward her like a poisonous reptile.

"I tell you, I'm not staying another day in this place. I can feel the evil . . . I'll go crazy—we all will! There's spirits here. They'll get us for sure! I'm movin' out. Take the horses and head east . . . bound to come to a well, or some kind of trail, a sand-dweller camp. Anything's better'n this."

"You really think we can find the trail—or water—without a guide? And what about our orders?"

"I'll risk it. And you better, too. You're just as scared as I am—I know you."

"What about the girl?"

"Leave her. She'll just slow us down, and we ain't got enough water. Better lose the pay than go crazy from evil spirits."

Chills ran through Meret's weary body. *I must stay awake*, she thought, *. . . stay awake no matter what. And if they try to abandon me, I—I'll fight for my life!*

CHAPTER 19

In the Sacred City, Bata returned to the busy square where he and Hector had agreed to meet. He carried Taweret, once more bundled up in her black cloak. Outside the sacred temple precinct—as he had discovered in the nick of time—she could no longer move invisibly.

Soon Hector appeared—to Bata's surprise, astride a horse. Close behind trudged a strong but gloomy-faced young man, a servant of the horse dealer, with two more horses in tow. All three animals were already laden with waterskins, blankets, and various packs. The man stood apart, holding the animals quiet, while Hector dismounted.

"Some luck at last!" he told Bata. "I ran into a couple of Greek officers—they didn't seem to guess who I am—who said it was probably a couple of Persian agents with some inside help. They're most likely heading east to the sea by the fastest route, and the palace guard's been sent out after them. The officers told me how to find the road—in case I want to chase the Persians, too, they said."

"Helpful of them," said Bata.

"Greeks stick together," Hector went on, without missing a beat. "So I went right ahead and got us fitted out. Did pretty well in the horse market—even got decent saddles. Picked up all the provisions I could, so we're ready to go." He paused, and frowned. "This has just about emptied my purse. I don't know what we'll do for money when these goods are gone, but . . . we'll find a way."

Then Hector looked pointedly at the bundle in Bata's arms. "Do you really have to bring your statue?"

"Yes. Of course I do."

"Why not leave it in a temple? The priests will guard it till you come back."

"No, I must keep it with me. That's the whole point." In a corner of Bata's mind lay some doubt as to how the goddess would fare in desert travel, but he tried to dismiss it. Probably no worse than himself. The very thought unnerved him, for having lived all his life in the fertile, flat delta, he felt fear of the desert in his very bones.

"Well, have it your way. But it won't exactly help." Hector shook his head in resignation. "What did you find out from your . . . your divine authorities?"

Bata spoke carefully. "I have learned from the deities that whoever has stolen the royal princess—"

"Whoever? Who else but the Persians?"

"That is not clear. Nothing is clear. But it seems she is held prisoner in a . . . place with white walls."

Hector sputtered with exasperation. "*White walls!* Well, that's just fine. And how much did you have to pay the priest for that choice bit of news? Hmm?"

"It wasn't a priest," said Bata, nettled. "There are other ways that the deities can help us."

The horse dealer's man, waiting with the two animals, coughed impatiently. Then Hector's horse stamped and blew, which alarmed Bata. He had never before even been close to such an awesome creature. Sparked by the animal's restlessness, Hector took command once more. "We can't stand around talking. Let's go!"

Now cold doubt filled Bata as he thought of what lay ahead. A reckless rush into the desert, a vague search for some white walls where they might—or might not—find the abducted princess. . . . Suddenly it sounded like utter folly. And supposing they did find her, how could they rescue her? Had Hector thought that through? Why, the whole idea was insane!

But then another thought answered his doubts. Wasn't this what he had come to the Sacred City to do? Find Princess Meret, no matter what might stand in the way, and present to her the gift of Pharaoh and his master Smendes? Besides, he couldn't possibly let Hector go alone. Whether madness inflicted by an evil spirit, or a gift from a deity with an odd sense of humor, a certain bond, Bata felt, had grown between them. Could this be friendship, between two such unlikely partners?

No, Bata could not abandon his purpose, even though he might very well fail, even die, in trying. If he chose the easy road, returning to Saïs and his safe but weary existence as a menial laborer, he would always know that in the one great challenge of his life, he had been found wanting. And most certainly, in the ultimate judgment of his heart, the gods would hold it harshly against him. He must choose the desert road, wherever it might lead.

Screwing up his courage, Bata loaded his bundles on the back of the third horse. Every time it lifted and put down a foot, he winced, and every time it gave a little shiver, he jumped. Although the gloomy-faced young man assured him that these animals were as gentle as sleeping kittens, to Bata they were almost as fearsome as sea monsters.

At last they were ready to leave. Hector mounted his horse and rode with confidence through the city streets, while Bata followed on foot and the young man led the two horses. On the eastern edge of the town, the man helped Bata clamber up on one of the horses. It was a struggle, especially as he had to hold on to the odd-shaped bundle containing the goddess. Once he was in place and grasping the rope of the other horse, the man left them.

Hector's horse proved spirited—obviously no sleeping kitten. That didn't seem to bother Hector, an accomplished rider. His spirits appeared to be rising: at last he was on the road to rescue the princess. But Bata, while admiring the Greek's skill, tensed with fear. What if the other two horses should try similar tricks?

Soon, however, Taweret's gentle voice reached him from inside her cloak. "These are good creatures, young Bata. They will do their best."

"Thank you, O Goddess," he answered softly, with great relief. Yes, she understood animals. . . . He recalled how the boat's cat had so often curled up peacefully next to the bundle containing the goddess. And indeed, the two horses did seem content to plod along obediently. Before long, Bata began to get used to the rhythm, and his fears lessened.

The trail got narrower and rougher as it wound through low, barren hills of yellowish sandy soil. An eroded landscape of hill and valley, the desert stretched on and on, with no vegetation other than an occasional solitary acacia or tamarisk tree.

Suddenly, however, the horses came to an abrupt stop. Below the raw edge where they stood lay a freshly carved ravine. A torrent had come pouring down the valley, gouging out the earth and destroying all traces of trail.

"Now what do we do?" groaned Hector. "That downpour yesterday—it must've been just as heavy in the desert." Nervously he scratched his head, then rubbed his short beard. "Maybe if we climb up the other side, we can see the trail from on top."

They coaxed the horses down across the soft earth and up a steep slope of newly eroded, crumbly soil. At the top they found themselves on a plateau that stretched far into the distance. Although there was no sign of a trail, the flat land looked like easy going.

Hector made a decision. "We'll just keep heading east. Sooner or later we're bound to come to the trail, or a well, or a stone quarry, or something that'll get us straightened out again." He spurred his horse on.

As Bata followed, Taweret again spoke from her perch in front of his saddle. "This is right, I think. I have no knowledge of the desert—far from it, for my home is the river. But I have the support of my sister deities, who will help to guide us through this desolate plain."

Her reassuring words kept Bata's spirits from foundering, for he felt utterly adrift in the sea of gravelly soil. As their shadows grew longer, however, cast by a pink sun descending behind them, he grew worried again. How could they spend the night in this wilderness?

The waning moon was starting to rise by the time they saw in the distance a cluster of spindly trees and a low-slung black tent. Surely that must mean a well. As they approached, four men emerged from the tent, wearing long garments of coarsely woven striped cloth. Bata slid off his horse, exhausted and sore, and tried to talk with them. The sand-dwellers, their dark faces weathered to leathery hardness, spoke few words of Egyptian but indicated that the travelers could stay. That was the law of the desert.

In his thin jacket, Bata would have suffered a bone-chilling night but for Taweret in her cloak, lying close to him. He marveled that what had originally been cold stone could now produce such a gentle warmth, and in the last moments before he dropped off to a fitful sleep, his heart filled with gratitude.

When morning came, Bata knew what he must do. Since Hector would object vigorously to the idea of seeking white walls, somehow Bata would have to find a way to win him over—without his knowing it.

Bata approached the sand-dwellers. "Do you know," he said slowly and very loudly so they would understand, "white walls?" His words met blank faces. Looking around, Bata spotted one of Hector's white undergarments peeping from a loosely tied bundle. He pulled it out farther, pointed at it vigorously, waved his arm around, and pointed up. "White, like this. Here, desert. White walls—high!"

Suddenly the idea seemed to click. The men huddled in conversation. Then, with worried looks on their faces, they turned back to Bata.

"We know white place," said one.

Bata's heart leapt. So there was a special white place in this desert!

"White place bad, bad. Demon."

Now Bata's heart quavered. Even if there were demons, however, he and Hector would still have to seek the mysterious place that the goddess Isis had foretold. But what if the men wouldn't tell him how to find it? He mulled over the problem, and soon an idea popped up. Maybe the sand-dwellers would give directions if they thought he wanted to avoid the evil spot.

"Where white?" he asked, looking fearful. He made gestures as though he wanted to take a roundabout route.

In unison, the men pointed toward the north. They seemed to know, all right. Glancing at the bundle containing Taweret, Bata caught a glimpse of one bright, knowing eye and felt reassured.

"What are they saying?" Hector demanded under his breath. "Why did they get all excited like that?"

Bata told him, "There is a place in this desert with white walls. They've given me some idea how to find it."

"Oh, come on! Are you still thinking of that story you got at the temple?"

"Yes," said Bata firmly. "The deities would not mislead us. These men say there is such a place, and they would know. But they think it's evil and we should avoid it."

"And that's where the princess is supposed to be? Excellent. This is crazy."

Bata had qualms, but he had to bring his idea into shape. "Wait. If people think these white walls are a place to stay away from, then . . . well, maybe it would be a good spot for the people who've stolen the princess to hide. Whoever they are, they don't want to be caught, do they?"

"Maybe they've already reached the sea."

That threw Bata off momentarily, but recalling their own journey, he had another thought. "The storm could have washed out the trail for them, too."

A light started to grow in Hector's eyes. "Hmm. Could be. If it rained hard out here, they might have to make camp for a while. And a spot that people avoid would be a good place to stay. Maybe we should try to find this—these white walls, if they're not too far out of our way." He turned on Bata with a warning look. "Not that I believe the princess is really there! But, well, we don't have any better leads."

Hector had made the decision. Bata nodded, then turned away to get the packs ready for the horses—but also to keep Hector from seeing the little grin on his face.

Their waterskins refilled, the three travelers soon set off. When they were out of the sand-dwellers' sight, they shifted direction and headed, Bata hoped, for the mysterious white walls. If the vision of Isis was true, he would gladly take on whatever demons might be lying in wait.

• • •

Although Bata was still unsettled by the vast spaces of the desert, he no longer felt so uneasy with the horses. By midday, however, both Bata and Hector were starting to slump, while the horses plodded more and more slowly.

Taweret encouraged Bata now and then. "I cannot tell you why or how," she murmured, "but I sense in my innermost being that we are on the right track. *Something* is drawing me onward."

Although Hector kept in the lead, he often turned and headed his horse back to Bata. "Are you *sure* we're going the right way? What makes you think so?"

"I don't know my way here any better than you do," Bata answered. "But I—I *feel* that it's right."

"Your divine goddess is telling you so?"

"Yes, you could say that."

"Oh, good. Splendid. That's just what we need—a statue giving us directions." In frustration, Hector would spur his steed forward again, soon to slow down and continue in resignation.

In the late afternoon a real storm blew up between Hector and Bata. Again the Greek took the offensive. "We're both out of our minds, Bata—and I'm the worst, believing in you! You're going to get us both dead in another day or so. Thirst or madness or both. You Egyptians and your magic, your tricks—you're famous for it. Infamous, I mean! Tricksters and charlatans!"

At last Bata's own temper snapped. "What do you mean? I have never played a trick on you—name just once!" Then, recalling how he had lured Hector into deciding to search for the white walls, he decided to take a different line. "If you don't like Egyptians, you don't have to stay in Egypt. You can go home right now. Go on, go!"

Hector nearly fell off his horse in surprise. "But I can't," he admitted. "I've got to find Meret. And I can't do it all alone."

"So stop shouting at me. I told you the goddess said the princess is inside some white walls in the desert, and we know there is such a place, so we just have to keep searching—"

With that, Hector yielded to despair. "Maybe it could be someplace really bad. Like a quarry, or a mine. Suppose she's been dumped in a quarry! Or— or—" A look of horror came over him. "What if this white place is really a tomb? Maybe she's already dead and turned into a mummy! By Zeus, if any harm has come to her, I'll kill every—"

"Hold it, hold it!" Bata said. "She can't be a mummy— it takes a long time to make a mummy. Don't imagine silly stuff, Hector. It confuses your heart too much. Just—just believe that you will find what you're looking for, and keep going."

"How can I help but imagine the worst? I'm a man of reason. And I swear, if Princess Meret has received so much as a scratch, I shall personally kill every Persian in Asia!" His face dark, Hector shook his fist. He gave his nervously pawing horse a kick and took off across the sands.

Maybe he really does love the royal princess, thought Bata. They say that love can make a man crazy.

Hector raced so far ahead that even on the flat plain, Bata lost sight of him. Time passed, and there was no sign of the Greek's return. Bata began to worry that his companion might have veered off in a different direction, or fallen into a hole, or even been seized by demons. As the sun declined, he grew increasingly anxious.

And then he saw, far off, a little puff of dust. To his relief it grew larger and larger, and Hector came tearing back.

"There's a fort up ahead!" Hector panted as he reined the horse sharply. "I saw it way off, on the horizon. Come on!"

With renewed hope, Bata got his horse to move a little faster, and they set off in the direction of the fort. The sun was near the western horizon when they reached their destination. But what they found was not a fort at all. A large, isolated uplift of grayish rock rose straight from the desert floor, so abruptly that it did appear to have been constructed by man rather than nature. Bata thought it must be about as high as the great walls of the Temple of Amun. Awe-inspiring . . . but not white.

At the edge of the rock, Hector turned back to Bata. "This is strange. It doesn't look natural. I'm going to explore. You wait here."

Hector rode slowly along the foot of the uplift—and then disappeared. Riding a little closer, Bata saw that there seemed to be a passageway into the rock.

Could this be the evil place that the sand-dwellers had warned them of? Bata was torn, half eager to reach the mysterious white walls and half fearful of what might be found there. Feeling the goddess move as they sat on the horse, he tried to hoist her into a more comfortable position.

"Something makes me feel we are close . . . ," she murmured.

At that moment Hector emerged from the break in the rock wall, leading his horse. Then he leapt astride and came at a gallop.

"It's white!" he shouted. "Brilliant, pure white! You get through that passage and you find yourself in a—a white place! High white walls—and a huge slope of white—like the snow on the mountains of the Lebanon. I couldn't believe my eyes!"

Bata's heart thudded. "So it's true!"

"Of course." Now Taweret's voice, although soft, had a ring of triumph. "Did not sweet Isis say so?"

"And somebody's camping inside there," Hector went on, his face aflame with excitement. "Just a few horses, no tents. That's why I got off my horse, so I wouldn't make noise—it's so silent, really weird. Bata, we're here! It must be the princess, it must be Meret in that camp. I told you we'd find her, I knew we could!"

Bata grinned. Of course. Did not the divine goddesses say so?

Hector's plan, as he explained it to Bata, was to leave his horse hidden behind one of the isolated towerlike rocks that rose on the wind-scoured floor within the white walls. Then he would stealthily approach the small camp at the base of the huge drift of sand. If Princess Meret was really held captive there, he would rescue her, somehow, and flee with her to his horse. If not, he would creep back to his horse and get out of there. Bata's role was to wait with the other two horses near the entrance to the passageway, ready for flight. Bata agreed that it was a plan so daring and so simple that it could hardly fail.

As Hector lay down to catch some sleep before the night's raid, Bata tried to make the goddess comfortable. Then he set out to explore the exterior of the rock uplift, curious to see what he could of the mysterious white walls. The rough wall seemed to rise nearly straight from the desert floor, with only a little stony debris at the foot. The rock was a grayish buff color, and there was not much of interest to see in the fast-fading light—until Bata came to a narrow cleft in the solid wall. Half filled with pure white sand, it appeared to rise at an angle toward the top.

Bata returned to the spot where the horses were tethered. When he described the sand-filled crack to the goddess, it interested her considerably.

"Remarkable!" she said. "The wonders of this world."

After the last glow had faded from the western skies, Hector set off. The night was dark. No stars glimmered, and the moon appeared only as a pale smudge through the clouds.

When Hector was out of sight, Taweret turned to Bata with a determined gleam in her eye. "Come, young Bata," she said firmly, "please take me to that crack in the wall you told me about."

"But, O Goddess," said Bata, "Hector may return soon and we must be here. The plan is—"

"I have my own plan," said Taweret, "and there's no time for discussion."

Filled with misgiving, Bata hoisted the goddess onto the horse, scrambled up into the saddle, and headed for the fissure. There's no arguing with a deity, he thought.

When they reached the crack, the goddess asked to be placed on solid ground. She pushed aside the folds of the cloak and stood. "Now, young Bata," she said, "let us climb."

He stared at her, wondering if he'd heard right. "O—O Goddess, but you can't! It's much too difficult."

"Quite so," she answered, unperturbed. "It will be exceedingly difficult for me. But my plan requires that I make this climb. And you did say that you wished to see the mysterious white walls, did you not?" Without waiting for a reply, she entered the sand-filled crack.

What could she possibly have in mind? Bata hoped the goddess was not suffering from addled wits, after all the hardship she had endured. He had no choice, however, but to follow, fearing that they would make very slow progress — if they could manage the climb at all.

Bata found climbing in loose sand hard enough for his long legs. For Taweret, the challenge seemed nearly impossible. She waddled and scrabbled, sometimes climbing upright on her lionlike legs, sometimes crawling on all fours. She slipped back almost as much as she moved forward. She did not reject Bata's boosts and shoves, but she would not let him carry her.

"I must get there by my own efforts," she said, puffing and gasping. "It won't work any other way . . . I'm sure of it."

"What won't work, O Goddess?" asked Bata, breathless himself.

All she would say was, "Wait and see."

Up and up they struggled, heaving for breath at every step. Although the lower part of the cleft rose at a gradual angle, it grew steadily steeper. More than once Bata cursed his curiosity, which had led to his discovering the fissure in the first place. He was getting as foolhardy as that Greek.

At one point the thought occurred to Bata that Taweret might be planning to ask the help of another deity, the way she had in the Sacred City. But that was clearly nonsense. There could not possibly be a temple anywhere around.

Almost to the top, Taweret flopped down on her swollen belly. "I am exhausted," she whispered. "I cannot take another step."

Now what should Bata do? Every minute counted. He had no idea how close Hector was to carrying out his dashing rescue, if indeed he had not already attempted it. Maybe he had been captured, or killed! No time to waste — Bata had to get back as quickly as possible. Yet here was the goddess lying on the sand, unable to move.

Controlling his impatience, Bata tried to speak in a hearty manner. "Of course you can do it, O Goddess. A moment's rest and you'll be on your way."

Taweret moaned, but she did not protest when Bata lifted her to her feet. After a worrisome moment, she whispered a few words. "Very well, onward."

At long last, Bata and Taweret reached the top of the rock. Here they found the sand lying in thick drifts, piles of gleaming white. Amazing! thought Bata, gazing around him in the luminous glow. Remembering Hector's descriptions of the mountains of the Lebanon, he wondered whether snow could look like this. After a moment, Taweret started slogging across the drifts, and Bata kept up with her.

Suddenly they found themselves overlooking a huge slope. Below lay a small camp, where a few shapes seemed to be moving about. Was Princess Meret really among them — and would Hector be able to reach her without being caught? Bata turned to ask Taweret what she thought.

But the goddess seemed totally oblivious of him. Sitting upright on the drifts of white sand, her head lifted, she seemed to be communicating with someone unseen. Gradually her voice grew more audible. Even though Bata thought he should not, he strained to listen.

"I have done what you required, O brother Min. Yes, every step of the way I climbed on my own feet. With only a little help now and then — only a little . . . !"

Bata listened, fascinated almost out of his senses. Taweret was actually speaking to the deity Min — god of the desert, of thunder and storm, of all things imbued with masculine power. And the things she was saying to him!

"Oh yes, my brother! I am thunderstruck by the magnificence of your domain. I can think of nowhere in all the Black Land that can rival it in majesty and beauty. The Nile, my very own home, is a mud puddle, a stinking swamp in comparison with the domain of the great god of the desert. Having seen the desert only once, I cannot imagine ever wanting to live anywhere else."

Taweret's voice rose, as though she felt the need of haste. "I leave it to you, brother Min. Do what you like, but do it quickly, please! And, O most honored, esteemed, talented, virile, and handsome Min, do call on me whenever I can do a favor for *you*!"

Her last words came in a rush — for now everything was starting to rush. A fierce wind had sprung up from nowhere. Bata's light jacket whipped about him, and he felt the sting of sand against his bare legs. All at once, the drifts lifted in great swirling clouds. The wind howled and whistled and buffeted Bata until he was afraid that he and Taweret might be blown over — or engulfed by sand.

Was this the deity's answer? Or the work of demons?

CHAPTER 20

Meret struggled to stay awake. Finally, exhausted and hungry, she drifted off to an uneasy sleep. She was dimly aware of activity, people moving about.

Then, with a start, she awoke. The night was dark, but the drift of white sand and the white walls gave off an eerie suffused light—just enough for her to see that the men were loading the three horses. They had folded up the blankets and rugs, piled them on the animals, and were now hastily tying on packs.

Groggily, Meret struggled to her feet. "Where—where are you going?" she asked in a tinny little voice that betrayed her alarm.

"Now, you just settle down and go back to sleep, Princess," Kai mumbled as he puttered with a strap. "Go on, just lie down again. Nobody's going nowhere."

"But what are you doing? I demand to know!"

"Now, now, lady, don't fret yourself! Nothin's going on. You just quiet down and—"

But as Meret realized that her fears were coming true, her dizziness turned to rage. She stumbled over to the nearest

horse and blindly started yanking at the packs strapped on
its back.

"You wretches!" she screeched. "You're trying to sneak
off!"

"Here, what're you doin'? Hey, leave that stuff alone!"

Meret yelled in fury. "You can't leave me here! I'll tear
everything off these horses—I'll tell Pharaoh—I won't let
you sneak off and leave me! You hateful cockroaches, you—"

As if in answer, she heard an unearthly shriek. A sudden
gust ripped away her words, and sand blew into her face.
Turning aside, she tried to protect her eyes as the wind
whipped around and tore at her clothing. She staggered
back to her blanket, groped for the headcloth, and managed
to wrap it around her head until only her eyes were
exposed.

The sand was rising more thickly with every passing
second. Stung and blinded, the horses reared in panic. As
the men tried to grab the ropes, the terrified animals pulled
away and bolted in different directions. Meret, shielding her
eyes, could only watch with horror. Without the horses,
they'd be lost, helpless! The men were howling like demons,
and the white sand swirled faster and faster, burning and
blinding. The night had turned to hell.

Her eyes shut tight, Meret heard her name being called.
Then again, and again—and in spite of herself, she felt compelled to answer.

"Here! Here I am!"

She forced open her eyes against the sand-filled wind.
To her surprise, she could now see quite clearly. Had the storm
passed on so quickly? No, a short distance away, the two
men were still struggling with all their might to hold on to
whatever they could. But right in front of her the wind
seemed much less fierce. How strange! A little hole in the
sandstorm, almost like magic.

Suddenly a large, threatening shape came pounding straight toward her. One of the horses! It would surely crush her—no time to dodge! But just in time, the horse jerked to a halt. Could she catch hold of it? Climb on and escape—?

No! Instead, something on the horse grasped her roughly, hauled her up, and slung her over the horse's neck. A moment later the animal was again galloping madly, and Meret squeezed her eyes shut in terror.

Then the howling of the wind dropped abruptly, as though they had reached some kind of shelter. The horse slowed to a steadier pace, and Meret felt herself dragged up to a sitting position. When she dared to open her eyes, all she could see was rock walls towering over her on either side.

A muffled voice spoke. "We're almost out of there . . ."

Her captor spoke Egyptian! Could it actually be an Egyptian soldier, sent to rescue her? May the gods be praised! Meret twisted around from her precarious perch to get a look.

No Egyptian soldier, but—that Greek!

"You! Is it really you?" she cried, her heart suddenly pounding.

"Yes, Meret, who else?"

"But—but—you're always bursting in on me!"

He let out a roar of laughter. He didn't explain, or say anything polite at all. He just howled with laughter, like an uncouth barbarian.

And then, as if one final mighty gust had blown all the sand out of Meret's wits, she understood. A miracle beyond imagining! Somehow Hector had learned what had happened to her, and somehow he'd found her. She sank back against him, heaving with spasms of laughter and sobs of relief at the same time. She even let him hold her tightly as he urged on the horse at a gallop.

Barely a moment later, they had passed through the wall of white rock. Her rescuer pulled the horse to a halt and it stood pawing, shifting this way and that.

"He's supposed to be here . . ."

"Who? What . . . ?" Meret asked, still half dazed.

"One horse is here—but where is *he?*"

Someone was missing. A guide? The anxiety in Hector's voice troubled Meret, and a chill went through her. Maybe she was not rescued after all.

CHAPTER 21

The sand swept down the enormous white slope in such a rush it threatened to bury the figures at its base. But at the top, strangely, where Bata stood braced and gasping, the wind soon relented. The stinging sand settled, and the air started to become clear again.

No time, though, to see what would happen next—Bata had to get back to the meeting spot quickly. As soon as Taweret appeared ready to leave, the two started floundering across the newly shifted sand to the cleft where they had made their way up.

The descent proved far quicker than the exhausting climb. As Taweret skidded along, she chirped and chuckled. "Who'd have thought it could work out so well? It was quite splendid—yes, truly splendid!"

But had it worked? Bata had no idea whether Hector had actually rescued the princess, or even whether she was there in the first place. He could only trust that Taweret knew—and she seemed more than satisfied. Yet he worried. What if Hector—with or without Princess Meret—should return, find Bata missing, and set off alone? They might spend the rest of the night searching for each other, or even lose one another altogether. Or . . . what if the abductors had managed to come in pursuit?

When Bata and Taweret reached the bottom of the fissure, they found no sign of a sandstorm outside the white walls. Fortunately, the good horse was waiting where they had left it, like a sleeping kitten. Bata lifted the goddess onto its back, then clambered up and headed for the meeting place. The exterior rock, weathered to its grayish desert color, did not give off the eerie light of the interior, and Bata strained to see in the moonless night. Soon, however, he made out the form of Hector astride his skittish horse.

As Bata drew near, he saw that Hector was not alone. A boy in coarse clothing sat on the horse just in front of him. At the sight, Bata felt as though his heart would crack. All that long, difficult journey—and no princess to show for it! Instead, Hector had carried off a common sand-dweller boy. How could he have made such a stupid mistake? Bata felt like pounding his head in despair.

Before he could say anything, though, Hector shouted, "We've done it, Bata, we've done it! But where were you? You were supposed to wait for me here. Never mind, we've got to get out of here, and fast! D'you realize, Bata? We've rescued her!"

But no, he *didn't* have the princess with him! That wasn't the princess. No princess could ever look like that. Hector must have been bewitched by the demons—there could be no other explanation. Dumb with amazement and dismay, Bata watched the Greek dismount, lift the sand-dweller boy down, and boost him up onto the third horse. *Now* what would they do, with Hector clearly under an evil spell?

The other two horses set off at a gallop, and Bata, holding Taweret, followed as fast as he could. His mind was spinning . . . he could not believe the disastrous result of their journey.

When at last Hector slowed the horses, Bata caught up and poured out his dismay.

"What happened? Wasn't the princess there? Why'd you bring *him* along?"

"Him?" Hector and the desert boy both turned to stare at Bata.

"Yes, *him!* We were searching for the royal princess, remember? And instead, you bring a miserable sand-dweller. Are you crazy? Are you bewitched?"

Hector broke into a loud laugh. "Bata, you fool, this *is* your princess!"

At that, the sand-dweller pulled off his head covering and sat up straighter in the saddle. Bata peered at him, closely and boldly—and suddenly gasped in astonishment. Despite the tousled short curls, the desert boy had the fine features of a girl—and the unmistakable carriage of a princess.

She smiled at him. "Yes, I am your princess, daughter of Pharaoh. And from the center of my heart, I thank you both for saving me. I shall thank you till the end of time."

Bata could barely keep from falling off his horse and throwing himself flat before her. He stayed in the saddle only because Hector was already urging the horses on again. Utterly agog, he trailed a short distance behind.

Taweret, meanwhile, half wrapped in her cloak and clinging to the horse's mane, seemed to be swelling with joy. "So we have our beautiful princess at last," she said. "Did I not tell you? Did I not bring you here, and climb the mountain, and overcome all manner of hardships to rescue her?"

"Oh yes, you did, O Goddess," Bata replied, still astounded. "You certainly did."

By the time the sun was above the horizon, they had left the white walls far behind. No one had followed them, but they were all starting to droop. Even the princess drooped, Bata noted in surprise. He was still too awed to think of her as an ordinary human.

Calculating their route by the course of the sun, the little group headed west toward the Nile. After some time they reached a small well, a hole in the ground surrounded by rocks, with a leather bucket on a long rope. They slid off their horses, exhausted, and Bata gently laid the goddess in the shade of a skinny acacia tree.

With a gallant flourish Hector poured some of the brackish well water into his brass cup and offered it to the princess. Then he took command. "Every minute counts, my friends. We must get back to Saïs with all possible speed, so Pharaoh will know the princess is safe — "

"And that it wasn't the Persians who abducted me!" the royal princess said in tones of indignation.

As Bata listened in astonishment, the story then unfolded. He could scarcely believe his ears. True, another part of the message from Isis had been proven correct. But to think that the Divine Wife, the revered and holy consort of Amun, could be guilty of such a crime! No, Bata could not believe it. Maybe, he thought, the princess was still in the grip of evil spirits, to say such things. He must lose no more time in presenting the goddess to her. She certainly needed divine protection.

At that point Hector interrupted Bata's thoughts. "We can't rest too long. Let's get moving again."

"No," said Bata, "we must do something first." Heedless of the stones, he threw himself on the ground before the princess.

"O most beautiful of sacred mortals," he mumbled, face to the earth. "O Royal Princess Meret, daughter of Pharaoh, I thy lowliest servant Bata do . . . do worship and serve thee forever." He hoped that was a good thing to say. His mind was half numb with fatigue, but he must try to present the goddess Taweret quickly and in a worthy manner.

Rising partway, he shuffled on his knees over to the tree where the goddess was resting. After removing her cloak, he picked her up reverently. Then back he shuffled to the princess, trying to achieve an appropriately abject posture without dropping his precious offering. Humbly he held Taweret out to her. He was only half aware that now the goddess felt stiff and cool, the way she had been in the workshop of Smendes: a statue, yet not too heavy for him to lift.

"O most gracious Princess," Bata went on, "may thy lowly servant Bata present to thee the gift of great Pharaoh — may he live forever — fashioned by the hands of lowly Bata's esteemed master Smendes, who — who worked very hard and did his most excellent work in the humble hope of pleasing thee and protecting thee — may thee live forever."

All the time Bata was making his speech, a nagging doubt pricked him. Taweret had started out as a stone statue. But now — he had long since given up trying to understand it — she was a real goddess. She spoke, slept, ate (or so he supposed), and very occasionally complained, and sometimes even talked with other deities. Shouldn't he present the princess to *her*?

In any event, he could not worry about it further. Princess Meret was exclaiming as though a star had fallen into her lap.

"Is this the statue that my father had made for me? The very same one?"

"It is," said Hector, nervous in his haste to get going again. "The very one. Bata brought it all this way. Now, I suggest that we — "

"He brought it to me — this boy? All the way from Saïs? Across the desert and — Why, I can't believe it!"

"You had better, it's true. And now—" Hector stopped short.

When Bata dared to raise his eyes to the royal personage, he saw her standing proudly in her coarse woolen garment, every fiber of her a princess. She spoke in ringing tones, like a crystal bell.

"I, Princess Meret, daughter of Pharaoh, do accept with gratitude the offering of this statue, this beautiful, beautiful statue of the goddess Taweret, gift of my father, fashioned by the illustrious Smendes, brought to me by this boy, Bata. And I do appoint Bata to continue as guardian of the goddess, entrusting to his worthy hands her care in all things. Rise, faithful Bata."

She laid her own hands, dirty but dainty, one upon the statue and the other on Bata's shoulder. Thrilled almost beyond enduring, he could barely remain upright on his knees.

Now, however, something else baffled him. To the princess, it appeared, Taweret was just a statue, carved of hard greenish black stone. Could it really be possible that she revealed herself as the true goddess only to Bata? Surely not. Surely, he decided, the goddess would make herself known to the princess in her own time, in her own way.

On the march again, Bata rode close to the other two for a while, still entranced at the thought of listening to a royal princess. By now, however, she seemed to be yielding to quite ordinary fatigue and spoke with a slight quaver.

"I'm so worried, Hector, about all the people who came with me—almost half the people in the palace."

"When we got to Thebes," said Hector, "there was no sign of the royal boats. We couldn't understand it."

"Those ruffians told me the boats were all seized and taken farther up the river, everyone a prisoner," answered the princess. "Tiaa won't like it one bit—I'll wager she's making life miserable for her guards."

Bata felt his heart grow agitated as he thought of the traitorous crimes in the Sacred City . . . for Taweret had assured him that Princess Meret's story was not the result of an evil spell, but the stark, scandalous truth. With dread he recalled the fury of the mob in the palace square, so easily ignited by wicked persons.

As Bata listened, the princess went on fretting about her royal flotilla. "As soon as we get back to the palace, I'll have Pharaoh send his army to rescue them."

"The army may be busy with other matters by then," said Hector soberly.

"Oh! Then we must hurry, Hector! Can't we go faster?" The royal voice grew high, and it drew a nervously irritable response from Hector.

"And how do you suggest we do that? All we can do, Meret, is get to some village on the river as quickly as we can. Then we'll take the first boat that stops—"

"We should go by horse," argued the princess. "The roads will be good at this time of year, and we'll go much faster. The messengers from the Sacred City will be making all possible speed."

Hector turned to her with an incredulous look. "Ride all the way to Saïs? Impossible. Our horses wouldn't make it even to the next town. No, the only way we can go is by boat, a fast one."

Bata encouraged his horse to move up and join them. This discussion was serious and involved them all. "Can't we command a boat for the princess?" he asked, and immediately wished he had not.

Hector threw him a withering glance. "Why, of course. And just in case anybody misses it, we'll send someone to

Thebes to report that the princess has escaped and is on her way back to Saïs. Bata, you'd better just tend to the statue."

"Oh really, Hector!" said the princess sharply. "He's just trying to be helpful. Don't act like that."

Bata's face burned with embarrassment. From then on, he kept his horse several lengths behind the other two. It seemed only respectful and kept him from making a fool of himself again. Besides, it allowed him to talk more freely with Taweret.

Finally the cool of evening fell, soon to be followed by the bone-chilling night. They came across no well or sand-dwellers' camp, just wasteland of dry yellow soil, with an occasional cluster of rocks as the plateau grew more rugged. Never a scrap of green.

Taweret slumped in her seat on the horse's neck, her massive head lolling. As the half-moon rose, she turned toward Bata. "I cannot hold on a moment longer," she told him quietly over the weary clop-clop of hooves. "We must stop, wherever we are, and rest for the night. We'll feel much better tomorrow, and I may even be strong enough to sense some water in these bleak surroundings. If we don't stop, I shall die."

"O Goddess, no!" Bata whispered in alarm. "I will give my own heart to save you."

"Calm yourself, young Bata," she replied with a sigh. "I was speaking for effect. I cannot die. But I can be rather disagreeable when tired, and if you want to spare yourself that, then we must stop for the night."

Bata called ahead to the others. While the princess was only too happy to stop, Hector threw back something about the Divine Wife's messengers, who definitely would not be sleeping. But spotting a low outcrop of sandstone that would offer some shelter from the wind, he agreed to set up a little camp there.

Morning came after a restless night, in which Bata feared that the growling of his empty stomach must have kept everyone awake. The travelers had eaten everything they'd brought, down to the last crumbs of rock-hard bread. Bleary-eyed, grubby, and painfully hungry, they got back on their horses.

For hours they journeyed onward under a cloudless sky and relentlessly bright sun. Bata gazed intently in the direction Ra always took, toward the west. There was no sign of the valley of the great Nile, not the slightest smudge of green. Nothing lay ahead but unending low, rolling hills of pale, dead brown.

Hector tried to rally the troops. "Keep on, friends! Somewhere there's bound to be a camp of desert people. We'll find a well, don't worry. There's cool water waiting for us somewhere ahead."

"Oh, do hold your tongue," said the princess, waspish in misery. "That kind of talk just makes it all the worse."

"I'm trying to keep up our spirits," replied Hector, peeved. "That's what a commanding officer is supposed to do."

"And who appointed you commanding officer? Thank you, we can do very well without one."

Hector lapsed into sullen silence, and no one spoke for a long time. Hour after hour they plodded over pebbly terrain, until they reached the edge of the plateau and started to descend slowly through winding gullies carved by rare but torrential rains.

Then, as Bata raised his burning eyes to the horizon, he saw green. Green! Could it be? No, not the river valley, just a small patch of green. But if it was really a desert spring, and not the deceiving work of an evil spirit, they would be saved.

Goading on their exhausted horses, the travelers arrived at the green spot—and the green did not vanish. Before their eyes a garden sprang up from the barren soil.

Most of the oasis was wild vegetation, tall sharp-edged grasses and thick bushes. Bata soon spotted, however, a small cultivated plot near a grove of spindly palms. Two farmers, nearly naked except for a strip of cloth around the loins, were tilling the dark soil. Mustering the last of his strength and taking care to cover Taweret, Bata rode up to them.

"Greetings, good fellows," he croaked. "We have lost our way and are nearly dead with thirst and hunger. Please tell me where we can find water."

"Water?" one of the peasants said in a broad country accent. "Plenty. Just up this path. But it's hot where it come out o' the ground. A demon lives up there, y'see, and to get the better of us, he makes the water hot. That's why we farm down here, where the water's run a ways and got cool."

"May the gods be praised," said Bata, about to collapse. "And . . . food?"

The men shook their heads. "We're poor farmers. We got barely enough to keep ourselves alive, until the crops are big."

By now Hector and the princess had also approached. The peasants regarded them with suspicious eyes. Hector, disheveled and dirty but still in the garb of a well-to-do Greek, and the princess once again concealed under the headcloth of a poor sand-dweller . . . they made a strange pair of travelers indeed.

"We have money," said Hector, holding out some Greek coins in his open palm. "We'll pay you well."

The farmers shrugged. "What good are those things to us? No, we got no food for you." They turned their backs and started hoeing again.

CHAPTER 22

Was there no way, Meret wondered in despair, to appeal to these peasants' mercy? Couldn't they see how near to starvation the poor desert wanderers were? There was plenty of grass for the horses, who were already drinking eagerly from the channel where the water ran down from the spring. But nothing at all for the humans—unless the two farmers could be persuaded to share their meager food.

Meret glanced down at her right hand. One finger still wore a ring, a handsome circlet of gold that had always fit tightly—and for that reason, probably, had not been stolen while she was unconscious. Impulsively, she worked it off, grimacing as it stuck at her knuckle. She knew she would regret losing the ring; it had been a gift from her father. But right now it could keep them from dropping with hunger. She held it out to the farmers, who were already looking on with interest.

Immediately Hector pounced. "What are you doing, Meret? Don't give them that—it's far too precious! Wait." He rushed over to his horse and started yanking things from his pack. The brass cup, his razor, a short cape: he flourished them before the two men.

They brushed him off. Having gotten a good look at Meret's gold ring, they had eyes for nothing else. It was the most beautiful thing they'd ever seen — and something they could trade for many months' provisions the next time they journeyed to town. One of the men ambled over to the corner of the field and soon returned with an odd-looking packet. Inside a large leaf, neatly folded, were bread, onions, and a soft cheese. Meret gave them the ring and accepted the packet of food. Too late, she realized that the ring was the only proof of her royal identity.

The three famished travelers limped over to a patch of sandy ground under a clump of palm trees, where Meret divided the food. Before eating, Hector removed the horses' saddles and gear so the animals could roll on the grass. Then Meret noticed that Bata had placed his share of food in front of the statue and was sitting nearby, staring into the distance. After a while, with a humble and grateful expression, he ate the morsels. How remarkable, thought Meret. Just as though he were a priest.

Hector now joined her. "You shouldn't have given them your ring, Meret," he grumbled. "What a waste."

"Why?" she said, irritated. "Because I might have gotten something better than onions and cheese for it later on?"

"No. Because it was your ring, your own beautiful ring. I always noticed it on your hand, so it must have been precious to you. You needed to keep it to . . . to remember, someday."

Meret winced inwardly. I haven't lost my ability to say the wrong thing, she thought. Then she spoke, with a little sigh. "Yes, you're right. I shall miss it. My father gave it to me. But we needed something to eat, and it was all I had."

"Greedy fools," Hector muttered. "They could have used my razor." He turned aside and ate in silence. Watching him, Meret could sense the humiliation he felt.

When they had finished the skimpy meal, Meret turned to another practical matter. "Since I cannot travel as a princess, I shall need a disguise."

His humor returning, Hector appraised her with a gleam in his eye. "Would you mind being a boy a little longer?"

"In these clothes, most definitely," she answered. "They scratch and smell. Whatever I am, I must have a bath first."

"Then you can be another Greek messenger — we Greeks generally travel in pairs. I think I've got one tunic left that isn't too dirty. How would that suit your royal presence?"

Meret smiled at him. "I accept your tunic with pleasure. And I will serve the Greek commander to the best of my ability . . . in my way."

Hector and Bata started to dam up the stream enough to create a temporary little pool for themselves, and Meret set off for a proper bath. With the tunic and Hector's second pair of sandals tucked under her arm, she followed the channel of spring water to its source. There, near the center of the small oasis, she found a large natural basin lined with stones. It was filled with hot water that bubbled out of the earth . . . and no sign of the demon. She lowered her aching body into the water and scrubbed herself with leaves from a plant growing nearby. Then she soaked blissfully, mulling over the events of the past days.

How rapidly her fortunes were changing! A pampered princess one moment, destined to become the most powerful woman in the land, and the next moment a despairing captive, fearing for her very life — only to be rescued roughly and carried off to . . . near starvation. What could possibly lie ahead?

And now, almost unbelievably, the statue of Taweret was with her! A little late, but at least it had been on the way. It was larger than she'd expected, but when she'd mentioned its heavy weight to Bata, all he'd said was, "The goddess finds ways to help."

In fact, that Bata certainly was a strange boy. Just the commonest of poor workers, without family or any kind of schooling, or even very sharp wits. Yet he seemed to have a quality that was decidedly not common. Hector had told her of the way they got to know each other . . . how typical of Hector to get into a scrap like that! So here they were, amazingly, and this poor boy Bata had gone through no end of hardship for her sake.

He seemed quite devoted to the statue, almost as if it were a living creature. To be sure, it was carved with astonishing skill. But still, it was just a piece of stone, simply a reminder to make people think of their religion. Hector, of course, thought religion was all nonsense. It was a wonder he tolerated Bata's taking such great care of the statue.

Oh, that Hector! So full of himself, so sure that whatever he said or did or thought was absolutely right. And yet, there seemed to be more to Hector than she'd thought earlier. She recalled the ring, and the way he had taken care of the horses first, famished as he was. If only they didn't argue so much! She could hardly say anything without his retorting, and she felt equally compelled to disagree with almost anything he said. Could he possibly really care for her?

And what could come of it, if he did? He was a foreigner, a wandering Greek who would someday move on to another distant shore. That is, if they survived *this*. Whereas she, Pharaoh's daughter, must remain in Egypt and serve her country. How could two such different fates be reconciled?

Then Meret recalled the moment of her rescue. She could feel Hector's arms around her again and hear him laugh in triumph and joy. She thought of his handsome gray eyes, the curve of his lips, his clean-cut jaw . . . even though his light beard was pretty scraggly by now. And she felt herself growing more warm than the hot spring water could account for.

As if to wash away all these perplexing questions, Meret slid lower into the water. Oh, how nice it would be to spend the whole afternoon in such comfort! But she had already lingered too long.

Back with her companions, Meret turned to display herself in the Greek tunic and sandals, her head covered in short curls. "How do I look?" she asked. "Would a Greek general entrust a secret message to me, Hector? Would an Egyptian boat captain give this foreigner a comfortable passage, Bata?"

"Without a doubt, my friend!" replied Hector, and "Oh, Princess!" mumbled Bata. Meret was pleased to see the admiration in their eyes.

While Meret helped Hector get the horses ready, Bata sought out the two farmers again. He returned with encouraging news. At a good pace they could easily reach a riverside town before noon the next day.

After leaving the small oasis, the travelers again found themselves swallowed up by a bleak landscape of eroded hills and gullies, with a fan-shaped outwash here and there. At least they now had a trail to follow and were sure of a destination. The next morning, as the rising sun sent her shadow ahead, Meret saw the beginning of green. Soon they reached the sharp line between desert and farmland, and Meret, however hungry and weary, felt overjoyed to be free from the grip of the desert. They were saved—but their journey was far from over.

As they made their way past fields of new barley, where shoots of brilliant green dotted the rich brown soil, they met a farmer. Bata asked directions to the nearest village.

"Straight ahead," the fellow answered. "Yep, there's a tavern, but it ain't like what you folks are used to. Where'd you come from, anyway?" He eyed them suspiciously. Why would two rich foreigners and their servant be wandering around the fields so far from any town?

Hector spoke in lofty tones. "Just a little excursion, my good man. No need to explain further. Now step aside, please."

Meret couldn't help a smile. One never knew what might come next from Hector—arrogance or good sense. This last speech sounded like both, and it seemed to work. The peasant shook his head at the foolishness of foreigners and set off on his plodding way.

The village turned out to be of good size, with a waterfront that looked as though some river traffic stopped there. Near the docks they found a tavern and learned that, yes, there were two small rooms empty. Payment in advance. The tavern owner was a hefty woman with a ready smile and masses of unkempt gray hair. She peered at the coins that Bata displayed in his broad palm and chose the biggest ones.

Comfort at last, thought Meret. But when she stepped into the room assigned to her, she looked around in dismay. At least in the desert she had had fresh air and clean sand, with all the stars and spirits of the heavens to watch over her. Here, by the light of one small, high window, she found herself in a tiny box hardly bigger than her jewelry chest in Saïs. At least it would be warmer at night, however, and they were soon served a meal of stewed fish that filled their aching stomachs.

By the next morning it appeared that the fish must have left its home in the Nile many days earlier, and the stew had done more harm than good. Meret and Bata wobbled and moaned, while Hector lay helpless in the room he shared with Bata. He called the other two in.

"My money's almost gone," he said feebly, "and we have to be ready to leave on the first boat we can get. By Zeus and Hades and all the rest, I may not live that long. You'll have to go out and sell the horses, Bata."

"I have to sell the horses?" Bata's voice was almost as weak as Hector's. His big feet shuffled nervously and his plain face creased with worry lines. "I've never sold anything, especially not a horse."

"Yes, you. I rubbed them down yesterday, before we had that . . . stew from hell." Hector groaned and turned away.

Meret, the least afflicted, could see that poor Bata needed all possible encouragement. "I'll go with you," she said. "And don't worry, these are good horses. They'll bring an excellent price." She chose to ignore the fact that the horses now looked almost as pathetic as their riders. Exchanging a glance with Hector, she knew he had no great illusions about them, either.

In the marketplace, Meret played the role of aristocratic young Greek tourist while Bata did the talking. First they approached a man, round as a turnip, who appeared to be a well-off merchant.

"Can't quite remember the last horse in this town," he said cheerfully. "We don't often see fine horses like what you've got there."

"Then, sir," said Bata, with a boldness and wit that surprised Meret, "here's a chance for you to own the finest horses in town."

The man roared with laughter. "What would I do with a horse? I can ride my donkey easier, and my oxen pull all the heavy loads. That's how we do it here. Take your horses to Saïs and sell them to Pharaoh for his army. He may need 'em, from what we hear."

Although the man's words alarmed her, Meret was careful not to react. Instead, she drew herself up proudly and looked offended at the man's rude laughter.

What he had said, however, proved true. Horses were not much wanted in that town. In the end, Bata succeeded in selling all three, but for less than half the value Hector had told them to expect. In addition to a purse of those foreign coins, which no villager quite trusted, the best they could get was three sacks of cracked wheat, four ducks already dressed, a large jar of honey, a basketful of vegetables and fruits, and a length of newly woven coarse linen. Meret cradled the heavy jar of honey in her arms, and Bata hired two boys to help him carry the rest of the goods. Later on, the food would probably be welcome. But would it pay for passage on a boat?

They made their way back to the tavern as quickly as possible. As they drew near, however, Meret felt a sudden warning. She recalled, in a flash of fear, the vague uneasiness she had felt in the Divine Wife's dark palace, and then, later, the sense she'd had that her captors were planning to abandon her. Something lay ahead . . . danger. A moment later, peering around a corner, she knew her premonition was right.

Two soldiers stood at the inn door, talking to someone. Clearly they were military men, but they were not wearing the colors or insignia of the royal army, which Meret knew so well. Who could they be?

Meret gestured frantically to Bata, who was laden with the ducks, linen, and vegetables. They both silently backed up and huddled against a crumbly mud-brick wall. Although no longer able to see the soldiers, they could easily hear voices.

"Nothin' wrong going on here, officers—this is a fine, legal tavern." That was the husky voice of the owner. "You got no business here."

"Now, now, sister," one of the soldiers answered in a soothing way. "Nobody's accusing you of anything. We're on a routine check, that's all. Just looking after the villages up and down the river. Just to make sure everything's all right, and nobody's causing trouble."

"So? Who'd cause trouble?"

"Why, nobody. But just in case—"

"Pharaoh looks after us. That's good enough for me. You fellows Pharaoh's men?"

"All you need to know is it's our job to see that nothing goes wrong. And *your* job is to help us."

"Me? How? You ain't making much sense."

By now this unseen conversation was definitely making sense to Meret. The rulers of the rebellious Sacred City were sending out agents as far as possible. Clearly they intended to undercut the river villages' loyalty to Pharaoh. And maybe more. Maybe they already had some suspicion that the royal princess was *not* on her way to a far distant shore, never to be seen again, but had somehow escaped.

One of the soldiers spoke again, his voice oily smooth. "All you have to do, sister, is watch for . . . well, anybody unusual who comes your way. You run a fine tavern, we can see that. Travelers would most likely come to your place for lodging or beer, wouldn't they? So you just keep track, and tell us about them."

"And by the way," the other man said. "Have you seen anyone these last few days, anyone . . . unusual?"

"You mean, like foreigners?"

"Could be. Or folks with foreign money."

"Or . . . maybe folks dressed funny?"

"Right. Not your usual river traffic."

"Hmm. Let me just think."

A pause, a moment of silence that almost seemed to shout. Meret strained to listen.

Then, "Yup, there's been some like that. Yup, sure has."

CHAPTER 23

Bata heard the princess gasp, so loudly he feared the soldiers, too, might hear her. She clapped a hand over her mouth and glanced up at him with a terrified look. He wanted to comfort her, but how could he, when he was just as scared—and his hands were full of plucked ducks? Scarcely breathing, they crouched against the peeling whitewash of the wall and listened.

"What's that?" said one of the soldiers eagerly. "You've seen somebody—like what we just said?"

"Yup. Right here at my inn." A note of self-righteous satisfaction sounded in the woman's coarse voice.

"Well, tell us, sister! Are they still here?"

"Right. Didn't get far."

"And . . . can you take us to them?"

"Shouldn't be too hard."

The soldiers seemed to be holding a short muttered conference. Then, "We need to know more about them. What do they look like?"

"Why, officers, just go down to the canal over there . . ."

"They're down at the canal—?"

"And bend over and look in."

"They're *drowned?*"

"Not exactly—"

"Then what, sister? What'll we see there? Speak up!"

"Why, you'll see yourselves! It's *you* fellows! You your-selves!" A squawk of high laughter rang out.

And then a snarled curse—"So you think you can make fun of us, old fool! We'll see about that! We'll be watching, you old bullock, and it won't be hard to close down your trash heap of a tavern." The furious soldiers marched off.

Bata and the princess could hear their tramping foot-steps all the way down the alley. Limp with relief and stifled laughter, they waited a little longer before venturing stealthily around to the front of the tavern. As they slipped inside, the tavern owner grabbed at Bata's arm.

"How long're you stayin' here?"

"We'll take the first boat we can—"

"You better! I don't want no trouble. This here's a fine legal tavern. It's all my dear dead husband left me—may he work in Paradise just as hard as he made me work here!—and I don't want them soldiers comin' back." The woman swiftly turned away, as if to pretend she had never seen them.

Muttering their thanks, Bata and the princess scurried to their rooms. After setting down the provisions, Bata went back to the tavern entrance to meet the two boys carrying the bags of cracked wheat. Soon all the goods he had acquired in exchange for the horses were safely stored away in the room that Bata and Hector shared.

As he found a good spot for the ducks, Bata heard a polite little cough just outside the room. Then the princess entered. "I managed to get some mare's milk, poor old Hector," she said. "See if you can get it down. With honey, it's said to be very good for an ailing stomach. We have lots of honey."

So the princess planned to look after Hector for a while, it appeared. Bata was glad. He wasn't especially eager to report the results of their horse sale.

And now he must look after the goddess. He found her silent and morose, resting quietly in one corner of the dismal cockroach-ridden little box that was Princess Meret's room. Getting down on his knees, he poured out the best speech of apology he could think of.

He concluded, "Ever since you came into my care, O Goddess, you have had to suffer. I feel terrible."

"That's enough, young Bata," she said, a bit distantly. "I know all about it. You don't need to remind me."

Chastened, he set before her a piece of good bread, plus two unbruised figs on a bed of long lettuce leaves. "May you eat well and regain your strength, O Goddess," he said softly. Then he squatted in another corner and allowed himself to drift upon a river of gloom.

Here they were, many days' travel from Saïs. Every hour wasted meant an hour of increasing danger for Egypt. They had to reach Pharaoh, as fast as humanly possible. But they were helpless until they could get passage on a boat—any kind of boat. And thus far there had been no boats at all.

As Bata brooded over their plight, he couldn't help recalling the high hopes with which he and Hector had set out from Saïs. How long ago that seemed! Now those hopes lay like a muddy mess. He sighed, his heart feeling as dark as a tomb.

"You are unhappy, young Bata," came the voice of the goddess from her shadowy corner.

"Yes," he said after another heart-emptying sigh. "This isn't at all the way I'd hoped. I'd wanted to present you— when you were a statue, I mean—to Princess Meret in a grand ceremony. I wanted everyone to see how beautiful you are, and rejoice that Princess Meret was under your special protection, and admire the work of my master. But it didn't turn out that way at all."

"Did you ever really think it could happen like that, young Bata?"

He snuffled a bit. "No. Of course I always knew better. They would have taken the statue from me at the kitchen gate and shooed me away. No, it was a dream that could not come true. But it was the only dream I ever had. And now everything has turned upside down, and we're stuck here in this awful place, tired and sick and scared."

"But," said Taweret gently, "since things are, as you say quite rightly, upside down, it turns out that you *have* presented your offering to the princess. Not only that, but you are still with your princess, protecting and helping her. She would have been lost without you."

Bata, however, was too far gone in misery to accept the truth of this. And his stomach was very empty. Tears rolled down his cheeks. Soon he was choking and sniffling, wiping his eyes and nose with the back of his hand. No woman had ever spoken to him as sweetly as Taweret did, and it only added another dimension to his grief. Besides, he was terribly embarrassed.

"I'm sorry . . . ," he blubbered.

"Never mind," said Taweret. "Tears are good. Remember, it was the Creator God's tears that produced humankind. Tears are the lot of humankind . . . and they cleanse the soul."

That night the travelers ate a light supper of broth in which a few pieces of turnip navigated listlessly. Then they settled down in their dank rooms. Bata again shared a small patch of straw-covered floor with Hector. Both were exhausted, and soon fell asleep.

A sudden rapping on the mud-brick wall woke them. Was it the middle of the night? Bata looked about, befuddled, and saw the pale light of early morning through the one small window. Then the raspy voice of the tavern keeper hit him like cold water.

"Git up—make it quick! There's a boat just docked. Go talk t' the captain—run!"

Faster than Bata would have dreamed possible, he and Hector were down at the dock, still rubbing their eyes. They soon spotted the captain, haggling with a man over a basket of meat. Hector, weak but putting up a good show, went straight to him.

"Have you room for three passengers, captain? Most important."

The captain, a short, wiry man, glanced at Hector askance. "Look, my fine fellow, this is a transport boat, stone from the quarries at Elephantine. What d'you think, I want *passengers?* No. 'Specially not young adventurers like you." He turned back to his examination of the meat.

Bata, desperate, stepped forward. "Please, captain, let me speak to you."

The man looked up, surprised at the boy's persistence. "Save your breath. My boat's got enough troubles. Hit a rock down there at Elephantine—no telling how long the patch will hold." Having evidently decided the meat was not good enough, he dismissed the seller with a flip of the hand and started to walk away.

Hurrying after the man, Bata touched his elbow. "My masters," he said in what he hoped was a confidential manner, "are messengers on their way to Pharaoh. They have very important news from the army in the Sacred City. They must travel secretly and as fast as possible. We have gone through much hardship, and we have very little. If you give us passage, sir, Pharaoh will be grateful to you. Please, you must believe me!"

The man scowled, and Bata fleetingly recalled Princess Meret's ring, bartered for onions and cheese. Would that have added credibility to his story?

"A likely tale," grumbled the captain. "How do I know a word of it is true?"

"My master is Hector, son of Leander, commander of the Greek forces in Saïs," said Bata, impressed at how smoothly the words rolled out of his mouth. "And his—his partner is also from a very important family. And they—we—have just come in all haste from the Sacred City, and there is great trouble there. Trouble for Pharaoh, trouble for all Egypt!"

As the boat master listened to Bata's words and studied the boy's face, his frown of skepticism faded. "You—you mean . . . ," he said haltingly as understanding dawned, "this has to do with . . . what we've been hearing about? War against the Persians?"

Bata was about to nod when Hector joined them.

"We cannot reveal our mission, captain," he said solemnly and in quite good Egyptian. "I'm sure you can understand the reason for that. But I swear to you, by all the gods everywhere, our mission is most urgent. Egypt's fate may hang upon it. We cannot wait for a passenger boat."

"And I can help Pharaoh by . . . by . . . well, yes! By all means! It is an honor." Suddenly the captain seemed to see Egypt's fate hanging upon him personally, and he was thrilled. He nearly bowed to both Hector and Bata, then turned businesslike. "Quick, get your things on board. We must be off as soon as possible."

When the already heavily laden craft cast free of the dock, it had four additional passengers. The boat, built for carrying stone, was wide and sturdy, its deck piled as high as a man's waist with rough-cut blocks of pink granite from the quarries in the south. All the captain could offer was a corner on top of a relatively level layer of stone, with a few wooden planks and some empty sacks for cushioning. In return, he was pleased to accept the four ducks, a sack of wheat, and some of the fruits and vegetables. Bata spread out the new linen for greater comfort. He hid the honey for an emergency.

Before the morning was over, the boat's crew all knew that they were carrying secret emissaries to Pharaoh. They regarded the passengers with awe and respect, even though rations had to be stretched further. But they couldn't help wondering. "Awful young, ain't they, them messengers?" Bata overheard the men muttering. "Oh well, that's the foreigners for you. No tellin' what goes on in their army."

Three days passed, long days of enforced idleness. With each day the crew seemed to grow more nervous and irritable. Bata had the sense that the boat was sitting lower in the water, but he couldn't be sure.

The three travelers, meanwhile, grew browner and leaner, and the princess really began to look like a boy. Bata never ceased wondering at her. How could a real princess, brought up in great luxury, having never done a moment's work in her life, endure such hardship? Yet somehow she did, and with rarely a word of complaint or a sour look. He longed to say something to her, to spread before her, like the finest feast, his reverence. But he knew it would be impossible. He would simply bumble and stumble and make a fool of himself. Sometimes he talked to Taweret, when they were alone, about his admiration for the princess. Taweret understood.

After several days of reclining motionless on her throne of fresh-quarried granite, however, Taweret was growing restless. One night Bata awoke to hear a faint sniveling sound.

"O Goddess," he whispered, "are you in trouble?"

"It's . . . nothing," she whispered back. "Nothing. I'm . . . nothing."

Bata sat up and, by the light of a mist-veiled moon, looked at her more closely. Two large, glistening tears were creeping from her bulbous eyes down either side of her snout. The sight squeezed Bata's heart.

"What do you mean, O Goddess? What can I do to help you?"

"Nothing. Nothing can help me. Since the dawn of time I have been what I am, an ugly old lump of a deity."

"Oh no, *no!* You are beautiful!" Shocked, Bata almost forgot to whisper. "Just as my good master saw you—beautiful."

"Thank you, young Bata, but I have no illusions," came the sad voice. "I am always a figure of curiosity, while my sisters—Isis, Hathor, Sekhmet, Maat, all of them—are loved for their beauty. And all my brothers—well, almost all of them—stand tall and handsome and confident of their power. I have my usefulness, true . . . but on this journey I've just been a helpless burden."

"No, that's not true," protested Bata stoutly. "You led us to the princess and to water. I know you did, even if you didn't say so. You take care of all of us, and you've been wonderful. Don't say those bad things."

In her dismal mood, however, Taweret wanted only to weep. Bata put his arm around her and let her weep to her heart's content. A deity should be allowed a little self-pity now and then, he thought. And in the morning, he could see that she felt much better.

But the morning also brought disaster. Suddenly the boat's crew started to rush around, peer over the sides, and tighten the ropes. Soon the boat began to tip. The clamor of panicky voices rose.

Dodging the frantic crew members, Bata found the captain. "What's wrong?"

The captain was tearing his few strands of kinky hair. "What's wrong? I'll tell you! That rock we hit at Elephantine – the patch is giving way and we're taking in water. I'll have to put you ashore at the next town – if we can make it that far!"

The sinking cargo boat crept around a broad bend in the river. It listed and creaked, barely wallowing through the water. As the boat tipped farther and farther, the crew kept tightening the ropes that secured the blocks of granite, all the time praying to every god in the universe. Bata and his companions sat nearly as still as the stone, scarcely daring to breathe, while the captain desperately coaxed his craft along.

And finally the prayers were answered. Around another bend a good-sized town came into view. No sooner had the boat been secured at the dock, than Bata leapt off with the still-wrapped Taweret and set her in a safe place. He returned for the rest of their possessions and what remained of the food supply, wondering what would happen when it was all gone. They had little left to barter, and they might face another long, agonizing wait.

This time, however, a boat came along soon, a large respectable-looking vessel with a load of fine textiles. Several passengers peered over the railing, which gave Bata hope that there might be decent accommodations on board.

The captain of the first vessel, however distraught, did not forget them. As soon as he was sure that his pink granite would not slide into the Nile, he called Bata to him. "I cannot neglect my duty to Egypt," he said. "I shall not abandon the messengers for whom Pharaoh is waiting. We shall talk with the captain of this boat. His name is Pramheb, and I have heard tell he is a good boat master."

But Captain Pramheb, who had the build of a heavy-weight wrestler, glowered as though ready to hurl himself at all comers. He plainly did not want any more passengers. A little earlier Bata had seen him talking with a woman on the dock, presumably bartering for some fresh provisions, but she had kept shaking her head. Maybe her refusal had put him in a sour mood.

"I've got enough on my hands," Pramheb snapped at the cargo boat master. "Got to make good speed to Memphis, can't hang around while fancy travelers take their time getting on board, demanding this and that. No, those passengers of yours will have to find another boat."

At the word "speed," Bata's ears pricked up. Taking a deep breath for courage, he said, "Respected captain, we're all ready, we won't keep you waiting, and we demand nothing. Please take us!"

The man shook his head and started to walk away — but not before the first boat master could grab his arm. "Not so fast, captain. You don't know who these passengers are." As Bata waited anxiously, the two men conferred in undertones.

Pramheb scowled beneath bristling black brows, scruti-nized Bata, and finally gave a resigned shrug. He would take them as far as he could, but they'd have to squeeze into a little bit of deck space and keep their wretched baggage from getting underfoot. The cargo boat captain, having done his best for Pharaoh and Egypt, wished Bata and his masters a quick journey.

The boat was soon under way again, carried along by the river's swift current. Hector, disgruntled at having had to barter his cloak, silver cloak fastener, and razor for their passage, leaned on the rail and brooded. The princess leaned with him, alternately comforting and chiding. Bata sat with Taweret on the deck, hoping that the jar of honey, which they had also used as payment, would somehow sweeten the captain's temper. There were no signs of it, however.

Taweret was uneasy. "Someone on this vessel is in trouble," she murmured.

"Everything looks orderly and peaceful, O Goddess," said Bata. "Please calm yourself. Maybe you just need a good rest after all the trouble you've been through."

She gave an uncharacteristic snort. "I've had more rest than I want lately. Young Bata, please don't contradict me. I know whereof I speak."

For a while, despite the deity's forebodings, the voyage proceeded smoothly. True to their role as secret emissaries, Hector and Princess Meret avoided the other passengers. They even declined some jovial merchants' invitation to join them in a jug of good wine from Crete.

Although the vessel was much less cramped than the boat full of granite, Captain Pramheb discouraged strolls along the deck. He himself prowled continuously, back and forth like a large cat in a cage, seemingly aimless and distracted. He spat orders at his crew and snarled at any passenger brave enough to speak to him. Occasionally he disappeared into a cubicle at the stern of the boat. But it was not to rest, because when he emerged, he always scowled more fiercely than ever.

The captain looked like a man with crime in his heart, thought Bata. By now he had an ominous feeling that the boat could not go much farther without something bad happening.

And he was right. The second night of their journey, a scream pierced the dark stillness. Then came another hideous cry, followed by whimpers and moans that made Bata's hair stand on end.

In a moment, half the passengers and crew members were milling around on the deck. Everyone muttered, gabbled, whinnied. "What was that? What's going on?"

Wild-eyed, flinging his arms about, Captain Pramheb charged among them. "Shut up and get out of here! Go back to sleep! It's none of your business!"

Bata saw with horror that the captain's hands were smeared with blood.

CHAPTER 24

Meret, who had somehow managed to sleep through the commotion, sat bolt upright. She stared groggily at Bata.

"*What*, Bata? What are you saying? I'm supposed to come somewhere? But why?"

"You will see—come quickly! O Princess!"

Scarcely comprehending, Meret struggled to her feet. Hastily she tried to smooth her tunic, then followed Bata. In the dim light, she could see that he was carrying something bulky—the statue of the goddess, wrapped as usual in that black cloak. He was pushing boldly through the nervous crowd that filled the deck. What could be the problem? It was so unlike Bata to be pushy.

When they reached the captain, who was wringing his hands and stomping around like a mad bull, Bata spoke. "Captain, my master will help your wife."

"She needs a woman!" blustered Pramheb.

"My master studies medicine," Bata went on, as Meret recoiled in astonishment. "He is almost as good as a woman."

What is he saying? thought Meret. What makes him think that? Sweet Isis, I can't possibly — Another horrifying scream tore through the night.

Bata turned to Meret, whispering urgently. "You will not be alone, O Princess — the goddess Taweret will be with you. She will take care of everything. But first you must go to the woman."

"Go!" shouted Pramheb suddenly. Before Meret could utter another word, he pushed her in front of him all the way to the cabin at the back end of the boat. Bata kept right on their heels and, with Meret, squeezed inside a tiny, stuffy wooden cubicle. There, by the light of a flickering oil lamp, to her horror Meret saw a woman in the torment of a difficult childbirth. The tumbled sheets were soaked with blood, and she writhed in pain.

The captain had stayed outside, cursing in his own agony. Meret was dimly aware that Bata had quickly unwrapped the statue and set it on a small table beside the woman. Then he backed out to the deck — and Meret was alone. Alone with a woman — and child — in certain danger of death.

What was she to do? What did she know of medicine? Or childbirth? Her thoughts were a panic-filled muddle.

In a moment's clarity, she recalled that ancient text on medicine that she had once read — long ago, it seemed — with such casual interest. Oh, if she had only studied it! But how could she have known? Then, like the first rays of sun over the horizon, a phrase from that text gleamed in her mind. *In treating patients, cleanliness can be beneficial. The doctor should avail himself of warm water for washing. . . .*

"Bring some water! Clean!" Meret shouted to whoever might be within hearing. She turned back to the suffering woman. But what next?

A large basin of water and some clean linen cloths appeared through the narrow door. The hands that brought them quickly disappeared. Meret scrubbed her own hands, then placed a wet cloth on the woman's forehead, wishing fervently that she knew more. In the palace, she had sometimes heard the screams of childbirth from the servants' quarters, but of course no one had ever explained to her what was going on. Not her concern, Tiaa had always said. And she had not even seen that horse in the palace stables.

Then, suddenly—she had no idea how it happened—she felt as though a wave of blissful warmth were flowing through her, carrying her above the terrible desperation that had clawed at her just moments earlier. She heard—she was scarcely aware of uttering them—words coming from her lips . . . words gentle, calm, almost like music.

"Breathe . . . breathe . . . steadily, slowly . . . I'm with you, I'm watching over you . . . you will be all right."

As Meret spoke in her quiet voice, the woman's high-pitched screams gradually lessened. Her cries and moans took on a steady rhythm. She huffed and groaned, but her efforts now seemed to have purpose behind them. Meret glanced at the statue of the goddess, seemingly smaller than she remembered it, but glowing in the erratic light. It almost looked to her as though the statue's eyes were upon her, knowing, approving.

For a few moments an unnatural silence fell, and Meret could hear the wails of the captain out on the deck. Then the woman started grunting and crying again, and Meret spoke soothingly, guiding her effort, guiding the child along its path. The goddess watched . . . Meret knew. And when she had to reach in for the child, pulling it out into the world, she knew that something holy was guiding her hands.

Finally, a new sound wafted from the tiny room into the heavy air outside, the thin cry of a baby.

And Meret shrieked. "A boy! A beautiful little boy! We did it, we did it!"

A moment later Captain Pramheb burst in, and bellows of joy echoed through the night.

Later, reliving the scene, Meret recalled a brief flurry when Bata had squeezed into the cabin and just as quickly slipped out again, taking the statue with him. Pramheb had been too delirious with happiness to notice.

As soon as he came to his wits, however, Captain Pramheb was a changed man. Restored to a more normal humor, he looked upon the young doctor in awe.

"Surely the gods sent you to me," he said in a gruff, trembling voice. "I knew my wife was in trouble—I tried to get a midwife at that town—I knew we couldn't reach Memphis in time—and then the gods sent you to me. May the heavens hear my thanks!"

For the rest of the trip, everyone on the boat buzzed about the birth of the boat master's child. The general agreement was that undoubtedly higher powers had brought the doctor to Captain Pramheb's boat and that each person on it shared in the divine blessing. Plenty of food and drink now came the way of the two messengers and their servant, even cloaks to cover them at night.

Meret bowed her head in recognition of the praise, but said nothing. For one thing, she had to keep reminding herself to be careful of her voice. Her shrieks, as a doctor, had not been those of a young man. So whenever spoken to, she said only a few words, in her very deepest tones.

She could do little, though, to conceal the amazement and rejoicing that swept over her every time she thought about that night. To help someone, she thought, to give someone courage and hope, and to know that her own hands made it possible! Could she possibly have the sacred gift for healing? Maybe she could study what had long been written down, but bring to it new ideas, new insight . . . because she was a woman. Oh, there was so much she could do in the world—she would never, ever, let anyone make her be the Divine Wife!

Once she turned to her companions, not to seek praise or even reassurance, but in hopes of letting some fresh air of understanding blow into her heart. "I still can't believe what happened," she said. "How could I possibly have done what I did?"

"You were wonderful, Meret," said Hector simply, his eyes filled with admiration.

"Yes," said Bata quietly. "And the goddess was with you, O Princess."

That just added to her inner turmoil. Meret looked at the two young men quizzically. Hector the doubter, Bata the believer. Then she glanced at their small pile of possessions on the deck, where the tattered black cloak covered the statue. And again, as she had on the fateful night in the captain's agony-filled cabin, she yielded to a mysterious calm. She knew that for all her life, she would remember those blessed minutes when a divine presence had guided her.

At last the boat reached Memphis, since ancient times the religious capital of the Two Kingdoms. Its wealthy population had a taste for fine goods, its priests did a booming business with the pilgrim trade, and its docks were crowded with boats going in both directions. Word spread quickly about the dramatic event on Captain Pramheb's boat, and many people came for a glimpse of the remarkable young doctor.

Pramheb, a persuasive man when he wanted to be, had no trouble finding a good boat that would take the Greeks and their servant all the way to Saïs, guaranteed. They soon boarded the craft, which was small, light, and carried no freight at all, just government officials. The captain, having been told only that his new passengers were highly significant fellows, looked puzzled but agreeable.

Meret stood by the boat's railing, watching the preparations to cast off. Right now, she thought, everything was going smoothly. But they still had at least three days' travel ahead of them. An image of her father came to her mind, and she recalled the evening when they had walked in the garden. He had tried to appear composed and confident, but his anxiety had been evident. Now what must he be going through? Constant worry over her safety, the difficult military decisions he must make under threat of betrayal. . . .

A wave of despair swept over Meret, and for a moment she shut her eyes as she clung to the smooth railing of the boat. When she opened them, she noticed a spurt of excitement on the dock below, which quickly diverted her attention. A late-arriving passenger was arguing with the captain.

"I have most urgent business in Saïs," he said, "and I just learned about the departure of this craft. I can pay more than the customary amount, even for deck passage. Come, come, my good man, you can see I'm a person of standing — you can be sure that this is no trivial matter."

"Deck passage is all you'll get anyway," grumbled the boat master. "And every bit of added weight slows us down, you know."

"I'll lend an arm at the oars, if need be," said the man with a hearty laugh. "May the gods bless you."

"Well, come aboard then, and make it quick."

So he, too, has urgent business in Saïs, thought Meret. *Very interesting indeed.*

CHAPTER 25

Bata missed the hubbub of Captain Pramheb's boat. He had liked the friendly merchants and their wives. Some had made a bit of a fuss over him, as the servant of the fine young doctor, and had given him sweet cakes and dates. On the new boat, the government officials were a dreary bunch. They spent their time seated cross-legged on the deck, writing reports or reading long scrolls of papyrus, occasionally playing a quiet game on a *senet* board.

Hector and the princess seemed subdued as well. Bata would have expected them to be excited as they drew nearer to Saïs, but the urgency of their mission appeared to be weighing on them more and more heavily. As Hector said, "The real challenge is just beginning. Getting into the royal palace won't be easy . . . not easy at all, looking the way we do."

Princess Meret said, "You don't look too bad, Hector. Maybe not exactly your best, but you look strong."

Bata didn't think Hector looked very strong. He himself certainly did not feel strong. For weeks they had had almost no exercise at all, just long days of weary riding through the desert, going without food, getting sick, and sitting idly on boats. He almost wished to be back in the sculptors' work-shop, lifting and lugging blocks of stone, using his muscles. But if the princess thought Hector looked good, who was Bata to argue?

As for Princess Meret, Bata could not resist staring at her every chance he got. She had grown slim and bronzed by the sun, and her curly black hair played in the breeze. By now she looked nearly as much like a handsome young Greek aristocrat as Hector did, minus the beard.

Bata was still puzzled, though, by whatever was going on between the princess and Hector. In a quiet moment one afternoon when the others were napping, he consulted Taweret.

"Hector told me, O Goddess, when we first decided to bring you to the Sacred City, that he was in love with the princess and wanted to marry her. Don't you think that's crazy?"

"Why should it be, young Bata?" she answered.

"But . . . he's Greek, and she's Egyptian. Pharaoh's daughter. Even if she's not going to be the Divine Wife, I don't see how he can marry her."

"The world is full of surprises," said Taweret.

Bata tried a different tack. "Hector was so sure of himself when we set out, as if he had no doubt she would love him as soon as he turned up. But it doesn't look that way to me. They argue a lot." Bata frowned, bewildered. He didn't really know how people were supposed to act when in love—other than crazy. Once, at festival time, he had heard a storyteller recite some poems about love that made it sound pretty complicated. But very interesting.

Taweret let out a little sigh. "It has not been easy for romance to flourish on this journey. Perfume and flowers usually quicken love better than do hunger and cockroaches. Although every case is different, of course. But more important,

Princess Meret hates the thought of losing her freedom. She has her own dreams . . . and any man who hopes to win her love would be wise to let her pursue them."

Bata wondered what Princess Meret's dreams could be, but it seemed an impertinence to inquire. Instead he asked, "Do you think she could ever love Hector?"

After a moment's thought, Taweret answered, "She will try to talk herself out of it as long as she can. She knows, after all, what a hothead he is and how much he likes to have his way. Perhaps she wants to be sure that he really cares for *her*, instead of just the idea of a princess." Again the goddess paused. "I hope he will prove true," she said softly, "for I think her heart is warm for him."

Any more of this conversation, Bata thought, and he would be completely befuddled. Besides, it was not his business. He touched the goddess respectfully on her humanlike shoulder. "Anyway, O Goddess, I am happy for *you*. You were so wonderful on Captain Pramheb's boat."

Taweret's huge jaws curved in a smile, and her bulging eyes glowed. "Oh yes! Wasn't that splendid? To help that poor woman through her travail—her first child, you know, and she almost twenty!—and then to see that sweet little baby, oh, it did my heart good. And Meret knew just what to do. Of course I was stretching the truth a bit when I told you to say that she was a student of medicine . . . but sometimes a deity has to take a few liberties. Princess or not, she's a fine, capable girl."

"Hector thought she was amazing," said Bata quietly, remembering the look on Hector's face.

Late the next afternoon, Bata found himself feeling at loose ends. The princess and Hector, seated on the deck, were engaged in a muttered conversation that drew serious frowns on their faces. All Bata could hear was references to the strength of the Persian forces, and he did not want to hear more. He got up and, keeping an eye on the bundle containing Taweret, leaned on the boat's railing.

After a few minutes, he happened to notice someone nearby: that late-arriving passenger who'd made a scene on the dock in Memphis. An amiable-looking person with a round chin and a well-fed belly under his expensive garment, the man now approached Bata in a friendly way.

"Your first time to Saïs?" he asked after the customary greetings.

"No, sir," Bata replied guardedly.

"Your masters . . . Greek, I assume? Yes, of course, what else could such handsome young men be? They are from the Greek camp in Saïs, presumably. Or the colony at Naucratis?"

"Yes," said Bata. "That's right."

"Well, well. Been traveling long?"

"Oh," said Bata, not sure how to answer, "long enough. We've been seeing the sights of Egypt."

For a minute or two the man gazed off across the flat lands of the delta, where a small half-ruined temple stood among grainfields. But before Bata, increasingly uneasy, could think of some pretext to leave, the man spoke again.

"You've been to the Sacred City, of course. You and the older of your two masters—Hector, I believe his name is. And the younger one's name? Me—"

"Me—Men—Mene-lus. It's hard for me to say those Greek names." Nearly caught! Bata felt a wave of cold go through him.

The man laughed and slapped Bata on the shoulder. "You're a good boy, Bata. Yes, I know that's your name— I've overheard you talking with your masters. Can't keep many secrets on a boat this small, can we?"

"I guess not," said Bata. This conversation was taxing.

"Tell you what, Bata," said the man, dropping his voice to a confidential murmur. "When you're back in Saïs, you may want to look around for . . . shall we say, something else. A smart, honest, hardworking lad like you — why, you could have your pick of good houses to work for. Or an apprenticeship with a fine craftsman. I might be able to help you."

Again taken aback, Bata stammered, "I don't think . . . I mean, I'm happy enough the way I am. But . . . thank you."

"Keep it in mind, my friend." With a wink and a fatherly pat on the shoulder, the man moved away. Bata watched him sit down with a couple of the officials and quickly become absorbed in their *senet* game.

Uneasy, Bata returned to his corner of the deck and sat down beside Taweret, concealed in her cloak. Then the princess joined them. She stretched elaborately and plunked herself down on the other side of the statue. Appearing to notice something wrong with her sandal, she stuck a foot in Bata's direction and leaned toward him.

"Look, Bata, I told you that thong was fraying, and you haven't done anything about it yet."

That was news to Bata. "I'm sorry. I don't remem —"

She leaned closer to him. "Look — you can see for yourself." Abruptly her voice dropped to a whisper. "Bata. Don't talk to that man again."

Bata kept still, hot with embarrassment as he tried to recall what he had said. Maybe nothing too bad, but . . . he really must be more careful. For the remainder of the trip, therefore, he spent most of his time sitting with Taweret, cramped and stiff.

The third evening, after the princess had fallen asleep in her corner, Hector sat down quietly near Bata. When he spoke, his hushed voice sounded full of reined-in emotion.

"Tomorrow we'll be there, and Meret will go back to being a princess. By Zeus, she astonishes me. She's so beautiful . . . but different from the way girls are supposed to be. . . . Her strength and courage—like a man's! I want so much to take care of her, make her happy. But how could she see anything in *me* but a—a jackass?"

It was an interesting question, and Bata gave it some thought. After a moment, he had an answer. "Well, I see the way she looks at you sometimes. . . . I don't think she'd look at a jackass that way. And remember when she fed you mare's milk and honey? I don't think she'd have done that if she didn't want to. Maybe she even liked it." The thought occurred to him that it might be good for even a princess to take care of somebody.

Hector turned to peer at Bata. "Really? You think so? Well, what should I do?"

Thinking fast, Bata answered, "Keep her hopes up. And listen to her."

"Even when she disagrees with me?"

"Yes. She's just as smart as you. And she wouldn't argue with you if she didn't want to be with you." With that profound and surprising insight, Bata thought how rarely he'd ever had a chance to argue with somebody in his life—besides the meaningless little squabbles in the street. It made argument seem very sweet to him.

Hector brooded for a moment, sitting knees to chin, then abruptly got up. "We'd better sleep now. We should reach Saïs in the morning."

A little later, as Bata tried to make the goddess comfortable for the night, she spoke softly. "I think what you said is true, young Bata. Nonetheless, I'm glad that you and I don't argue. It's not your way, nor mine. Now let us follow your friend's advice and rest. There's no telling what the morrow will bring us."

CHAPTER 26

The next morning, on schedule, the boat reached Saïs. Meret felt her heart start to beat with impatience and apprehension. Almost home—yet the climax of the trip was still to come. As soon as they stepped on dry land, they would have to make a breakneck dash for the palace.

As the eight oarsmen maneuvered the boat up to the dock, Meret watched at the rail with Hector and Bata. The waterfront bustled with activity . . . but it was a strange crowd. Soldiers everywhere, Egyptian and Greek. Evidently several divisions had just reached Saïs from other parts of the country. The foreigners' tunics and heavy armor contrasted with the short kilts, spears, and leather shields favored by the Egyptians. Tension seemed to radiate between the Egyptian and Greek troops. In separate ranks but too near one another for comfort, the warriors looked as jittery as alley cats, either itching for combat or terrified of it.

The restive atmosphere distressed Meret. "So different from the last time I saw this place," she murmured sadly. "Such a hullabaloo then, and everybody so happy. All except me, that is. And now it looks so grim. What is going to happen?"

With unusual boldness, Bata sought to comfort her. "It will be all right, O—master. As soon as we reach where we're going."

"We hope," said Hector, worry lines in his forehead. "We hope. Wish we knew how long it took the messengers from Thebes to get here. For sure they traveled faster than we could. I just hope a few cool heads—"

He stopped short. Glancing up, Meret saw that they had company: the gentleman with urgent business in Saïs. He smiled affably. "Pretty exciting, isn't it, getting home after a long trip. Someone here to meet you young gentlemen?"

"We can manage, thanks," said Hector quickly.

The man went right on. "Let me help you—I know the capital very well indeed. You just stick close to me, and I'll see that you find a porter. Now don't you worry, just leave it all to me."

Meret exchanged an apprehensive look with Hector. He was starting to protest—"Thanks, but—" when the boat hit the dock with a jolt that shook them all off balance. The captain cursed at the oarsmen, other crew members slid the gangplank down to the dock, porters started shouting for business, and the government officials all began chattering among themselves.

"We've got to get out of here, and fast!" Hector muttered. He and Meret seized what they could of their few remaining bundles, and Bata grabbed the statue.

With Meret between himself and Bata, Hector elbowed his way among the disembarking passengers, who glared and snapped at the three young people. As they hustled down the gangplank, Meret felt herself pushed from behind. Half turning, she saw that Bata, propelled by the weight of the statue, had nearly lost his balance. He gasped a word of apology, and they both hurried on, following close

CHAPTER 26 **191**

behind Hector through the crowds of officials, vendors, and porters on the dock.

But hardly had they taken a few steps when the friendly gentleman from the boat seemed to pop up from nowhere. All three had to stop short to avoid crashing into him.

"What's this?" the man said in breathless joviality. "I told you to let me help you. Don't be shy! Here, let me call a porter." He pulled a small whistle from the folds of his garment and quickly blew a series of short notes.

Instantly three large, beefy men appeared, wearing the tattered loincloths of porters. Instead of reaching for the travelers' bundles, one shoved Hector and Bata out of the way and the other two pressed close to Meret. Each grabbing an arm, they started to drag her through the milling crowd. Meret yelled in alarm and defiance, and a high laugh rose above the waterfront hubbub.

"Sorry, Princess—but we must do it this way!"

CHAPTER 27

It happened so fast, Bata could barely comprehend what was going on. Frantically, he looked around. So many people—where was Hector? Could he do something, or had he—?

Then Bata caught sight of the princess, twisting and struggling in the grip of the two supposed porters. She let out another piercing yell, and a shout answered—in Greek, but the meaning was clear.

"Swine, let her go!"

Crimson-faced with rage, Hector dashed at the men. He took a fierce swing and connected with a burly midsection. While it didn't appear to hurt the man at all, it surprised him and threw him off stride. Taking advantage, Hector swung again and again, pounding wherever he could. But it was a losing effort. The men were much larger, and there were more of them. In a moment, the third man tossed Hector aside as though he were a yapping little dog.

Bata watched, horrified. His muscles responded—he wanted desperately to tackle the brutes as they dragged the struggling princess along. But how could he, holding the goddess?

Hector yelled again. Up on his feet once more, he threw himself at one of the men and got in a few quick blows. Bata's dismay now changed to awe. Hector was fighting! Just as before, however, the man shook him off easily. Down he went again.

"O Goddess, we've got to help!" Bata gasped.

"Absolutely," came the quick reply. But what could they possibly do against such odds?

Suddenly Bata recalled the rush down the gangplank, and how the weight of the goddess had made him move faster. Holding her to his chest even more tightly, he lowered his head and ran full tilt at the men. His head smashed into a body, and he heard an outraged howl as two of the men crashed into each other. In the next instant, though, a burly arm caught him in the face, and he found himself thrown down. Big as he was, he could do no better than Hector.

Would they lose the princess, so close to their goal? Bata's eyes bleared with tears of anger and frustration as he struggled to his feet, still managing to keep a firm grip on the goddess.

Just then, a new cry rose above the portside hubbub. Twisting around, Bata saw that a group of Greek soldiers had broken ranks and were rushing toward them. Hector shouted to the Greeks. Several set off for the abductors, who by now were hampered by a growing crowd. Catching up, the Greek soldiers seized and beat the men until they lost their hold on the princess. Hector rushed back into the fray, grabbed her, and yelled for Bata to follow.

The fight was not over. Now Egyptian soldiers, too, were falling out of their ranks. Adding their own shouts, they made for the Greeks.

Ducking and dodging, the princess and the two boys slipped among the armored bodies and made their escape.

Bata looked back, just before he rounded a corner into a maze of waterfront buildings and alleys. The whole dock-side, simmering with tension, had boiled over into battle. Greek against Egyptian, native against foreigner, the soldiers fought like men with no idea of the cause, only the instinct of mob passion. Again a fleeting recollection of the hysteria in the Sacred City passed through Bata's mind.

The shouts and thuds of the waterfront fight faded behind him as Bata hustled down an alley between close-packed buildings. Ahead, Hector paused for a moment, waiting for him to catch up. With Princess Meret by the hand, he called, "Hurry! They may have men all over the town!"

"I'm doing the best I can!" Taweret's weight had given Bata momentum in the fight, but now he was finding it hard to run fast.

Up one alley and down another, right turns, left turns, once even backtracking, the three raced along. Bata was surprised to find the small marketplaces nearly empty. Instead of the usual hubbub, an uncanny silence hung over the quarter. The few people they met seemed to take no notice of them, turning away as they rushed past. Saïs looked like a town taken over by the military, where the people could expect only trouble ahead.

Gradually the dense housing gave way to better residences. All were tightly closed, with shuttered windows. Then, almost abruptly, the narrow streets opened into a large, well-paved plaza. Ahead of them rose the palace, three lofty stories of gleaming whitewashed brick surrounded by a high, thick wall. The magnificent gate of brilliantly polished stone was well guarded.

"No use trying this gate—it's just for ceremonies," gasped the princess, breathless from her run. Her tunic was torn, her face reddened on one side. She must have been struck when the men were trying to drag her off, Bata thought, chagrined that he and Taweret had not been able to protect her when she most needed it.

"Come—this way—we'll find a smaller gate." She ran ahead down a side street. This gave Bata his first chance to speak to Hector, as they hurried along behind.

"You fought like a great warrior, Hector!"

Hector stopped short and looked at Bata in pleased surprise. "I did? Really? Well, of course!"

A moment later, they caught up with Princess Meret and approached the plaza from a different side. Ahead of them, at a smaller gate in the palace wall, stood two soldiers at attention. Again Hector took the lead, walking with a swift, confident pace. The princess followed, and Bata hustled along behind them, struggling with one end of Taweret's cloak that was now trailing in the dust.

Then Hector paused, muttering, "Bad luck. I don't think these guards know me. Well, can't be helped." Striding up to the guards, who stood on a small platform, he planted himself firmly. The men barely glanced down at him and then stared off into the distance, as though these three shabby ruffians were not even worth sending away with a few curses.

"We request admittance to the palace," announced Hector, catching his breath. "We are here on urgent business. Let us in immediately, please."

At this, one guard lowered his gaze a bit. "And who might you be, my fine fellow?"

"I am Hector, son of Leander. Let me pass—and my companions. I repeat, this is urgent business."

"Son of Leander? You expect us to believe that, little street brawler?"

Bata wasn't surprised at the guard's reaction. Hector's formerly white tunic was stained all over, his tousled hair stood on end, and he bore obvious signs of battle. A dark bruise was already spreading on his arm, dried blood marked a split lip, one eye was swollen nearly shut. The princess, although less damaged, was equally dirty and disheveled. Again Bata recalled her ring, the royal ring that might have made it easy for them to be admitted.

Hector pulled himself up taller. "Yes, indeed!" he declared. "Come, we can't waste time—"

"Hector, son of Leander," the guard repeated. "Very interesting. Prove it."

"Go call General Leander. Call any of the Greek officers—they all know me. And make it quick."

"Too bad. They're all busy with slightly more important matters. High command council—" He broke off as the other guard took a step toward him, gestured at the once-fine Greek tunics worn by Hector and the princess, and muttered a few words of advice. Reluctantly, the first guard then turned back to Hector.

"Go on," he said brusquely, with a backward jerk of the head. "Let them handle it inside. If you're not who you say you are, you'll get booted out faster than you can spit." Then his glance fell on the princess, and a slight grin returned to his face. "What about you, handsome? You're the missing princess, I suppose."

Princess Meret drew herself up disdainfully, a deep flush darkening her smudged cheeks. Hector shoved her and Bata through the gate as soon as the guards stepped aside, and they hurried up a flight of stone steps before the men could change their minds. Reaching the top, they confronted a pair of large bronze doors. At a shout from the outer guard, the doors slowly swung open.

Inside the building, light filtered down from a row of high windows. Bata paused to gawk at the walls, glowing white with flowers painted in gorgeous shades of blue, crimson, and green. The floor, too, was covered with floral designs. In a moment, they arrived at another set of closed doors, made of intricately inlaid wood. The two guards by these doors were dressed in ceremonial regalia: elaborate bronze breastplates and helmets, spears, and shields that looked more ornamental than practical.

Hector repeated his demand. "If you need proof that I'm who I say I am, let me tell you about the Greek high command. General Hippias has a broken nose, crooked as a folding chair. . . . Commander Lycurgus's hands are as white as a woman's. . . . Lieutenant Agathon belches every time he speaks. . . ."

These observations seemed to carry some weight with the guards. "You may enter," one said to Hector. "But the other two, no. How do we know who they are? They'll have to wait in another part of the palace until you've been questioned further."

The princess started to protest, then kept silent. The doors swung open and a guard appeared, taking Hector—none too gently—by the arm. He had barely time for a glance back at his companions before he was pulled inside.

At the same moment, another guard arrived to take charge of Bata and the princess. A tall, burly man, he clapped large hands on their shoulders, spun them around, and propelled them swiftly down the dim corridor, where at intervals flames from tall brass braziers threw eerie shadows across the patterned walls. Bata was infuriated to see the princess forced to run like a child being hurried along by an impatient mother. Even he, with his long legs, could barely keep up with the guard's pace, and he kept stepping on the trailing cloak.

To make matters worse, Taweret was starting to twitch. Of course she was uncomfortable, but what could Bata do? He found it hard to keep a good grip on her, she wiggled so. Did she want to say something? Impossible! But the goddess kept kicking until Bata managed to bend his head enough to hear.

"Unwrap me and let me down—quickly!" Surely she didn't think she could escape by herself? Yet she kicked again, even more urgently.

At that moment, as they were being steered around a corner, the princess stumbled and the guard had to slow a little. Bata managed to drop the cloak and lean forward enough to set the goddess down. With a crack like the sound of shattering glass, Taweret's tail came detached from her lower back—and whipped across the guard's ankle. Losing his balance, he let go of his two captives and fell heavily against the tall thin legs of a brazier. Over it went, splashing the burning oil. The guard howled as if demons had set upon him.

"What happened?" gasped the princess. "Bata, did you fall? Is the statue all right?"

"Yes, it is—I dropped the cloak, and the guard must have tripped—" Bata answered, panting.

"Good! Now follow me!"

Bata grabbed up Taweret again as the princess started to run down the darkened hallway, up one short flight of stairs and down another, across a wide empty hall, through a narrow dark passage. Bata lumbered along as fast as he could. He grew dizzy, trying to keep focused on the slim back of the princess as they raced along.

And Taweret was still wiggling. Her voice, hushed but jubilant, came close to his ear. "I did it! I got my tail loose— and just in time!" So that explained the struggle! Taweret, by her own efforts, had finished what Smendes could not.

But there was no time for admiration. Just ahead, the princess paused for a moment. "We're going a roundabout way, so they can't catch us," she whispered. "Don't worry, I know the palace!"

On they ran. A couple of times they spotted guards, but the princess ducked behind a flight of stairs or into a small closet, then set off in a different direction. At last they reached a chamber that appeared to be part of the living quarters. Bata caught a glimpse of chests and chairs. The princess dashed through, opened a door at the far end, and entered a dark tunnel. Here there was no light at all. With one hand, Bata groped his way along gingerly. He and Taweret bumped into the princess when she stopped again.

"It's a secret passage from Pharaoh's chambers to the council room," she whispered. "He showed me when I was little—and thanks to the gods, I've remembered it. Now, if only it's unlocked at the other end . . ."

They continued with caution and suddenly all piled up against an unseen door. Bata could hear Princess Meret mutter as she felt its surface and found a handle. It moved. The hinges let out a squeal of protest and then, as the door opened farther, made no more sound.

"It must have been oiled," she murmured. "He never liked to use it. Now it's ready, in case . . ."

From the blackness of the tunnel, Bata and the princess emerged into an antechamber, a small stark room lit faintly by an overhead opening. Before them stood one more door. They heard voices within—many voices, loud and forceful. Bata could hardly control a shiver of fear as he looked questioningly at the princess in the dim light.

"The innermost council room," she whispered. "Pharaoh must be meeting with all the Egyptian and Greek generals. I think the door will be unlocked—I hope so!"

"Then—then what?"

But she was already easing the door open, revealing a heavy curtain over the entrance. Did she plan simply to dash right in—among Egypt's king and all those angry-sounding generals?

"Wait, O Princess!" Bata whispered urgently. "What should I do?"

"You just follow me. They'll be so happy to see—"

The curtain flew open, and a blaze of light half-blinded Bata. Against the brightness loomed a large, dark shape.

"Spies!" The guard seized Bata and dragged him into the room.

Clutching the goddess for dear life, Bata stumbled into the midst of a large circle. He could barely comprehend what he was seeing, his eyes dazzled by the fire of many oil lamps and the glistening of armor. The next instant he was hurled to the floor. Twisting as he fell, he managed to take the force of the fall on his side. The goddess was not hurt.

For a moment Bata could only lie there, his eyes squeezed shut, his chest heaving. He could hear the cries all around him, the ominous growl of fury. Booted feet ringed him — and he could sense the spears thrust at him, just a hand's length away. He lay there with Taweret in his arms, once more hard and cold — but safe.

Then one voice rose above the others. "He's holding something . . . What is it? What does he have? Stand back, guards! Pharaoh wants to see."

A new burst of furious cries — "A statue! Thief, thief! Beat him — kill him!"

I must . . . must give the goddess to Pharaoh, thought Bata. With his last strength, he managed to get on his knees. Then he held up the goddess. A hush of astonishment fell on the room. Bata's head was still bowed, his eyes fixed on the precious object in his arms, and his voice trembled. But his words came out.

"O Pharaoh, here is the statue of the goddess, Taweret, made by my master Smendes. I have brought her to —"

A body thudded to the floor beside him. He turned, horrified, to see the princess lying there motionless. Then, with a wrenching effort, she managed to lift her head.

"Pharaoh — Father!" she gasped. "I am Princess Meret, your daughter! I'm all right, I've come home! Believe me, *please* . . . oh, you must believe me!"

More uproar, shouts of amazement, cries of disbelief. And again, one voice rose above the rest. Someone rushed forward, someone lifted the princess to her feet. Bata saw the shining white robes of a man just a short distance in front of him, but he could not raise his eyes higher.

In the sudden silence, Pharaoh whispered, "Can it be? Can this be my daughter Meret, my beloved daughter, whom I thought never to see again?"

"Yes, Father, yes! Oh, I've had such a time—"

She got no further, for someone else had just burst into the room and another voice boomed out. "Hector, son of General Leander!"

Bata, clutching the statue, sank back on his heels and looked up as Hector, still filthy and battered but unmistakably the son of Leander, strode into the circle. He went first to Pharaoh and bowed low, then stepped over to a man whose tall, august figure seemed to dominate all the other armored bodies in the room, and saluted. Then he turned to the whole assembly and spoke in a firm voice.

"We have returned from the Sacred City. Princess Meret is restored to you, safe and well. But Egypt must beware—"

And everything else washed over Bata like the Nile in flood. He heard the joy, the outrage, the relief . . . and at one point he heard a loud, clear order ring out, followed by a resounding cheer. But words were beyond him. He stayed on the floor, kneeling, while the room whirled about him. After a while, someone came and respectfully picked up Taweret. Two persons, in fact, and with difficulty. But before they took her away, her head turned slightly toward Bata. He saw the soft gleam in her eye, and he knew it was meant for him alone.

And he knew, too, that he had carried out his master's last order: *Finish my work.*

CHAPTER 28

The palace seemed uncommonly quiet as Meret and her father enjoyed the balmy air of a spring afternoon in the garden. On the one hand, Meret was pleased not to have a flock of servants hovering around her. Somehow, she proudly told her father, she had managed quite nicely by herself in the desert.

Yet the very absence of all those servants worried her. What was happening to that captive flotilla, moored somewhere south of the Sacred City?

Earlier, Pharaoh had told her that troops were on their way by the fastest boats, to find and rescue the royal fleet. "And it won't be long," he'd added, "before you have your beloved Tiaa back." Meret had mixed feelings at that remark. Certainly at times she'd wished to have Tiaa around to make everything all right again—but how she had loved being on her own!

Meanwhile, here she was again in her own home, walking once more with her father in the same garden where they had made that fateful decision, ages ago, it seemed. At last they could talk frankly about the traitorous Sacred City.

"I think," said Meret soberly, "the Divine Wife must be

in conspiracy with the Persians. She must believe that if they take over Egypt, they will let her keep all her wealth—and maybe more—as a reward for betraying you. What madness! Don't you think so, Father?"

A faint smile crossed Pharaoh's lips, and then he sighed. "It is true. When a person with power has no responsibility for the betterment of others, it does lead to madness. Egypt's kings have always been guided by the great Wisdom writings that show us the straight path; but in the case of the Divine Wife, I'm not sure there is such a guide."

"Well, are you going to send me back there?" Meret's voice was light, but her question serious, for clearly a loyal Divine Wife would strengthen the throne. At the same time, she was more resolved than ever not to let it happen.

The look her father cast on her was both kindly and rueful. "No, my daughter, have no fear of that. Such a decision may well be taken out of our hands."

The Persians . . . the ever-present menace poised in the east. By reaching Pharaoh in time, Meret and her companions had prevented an Egyptian offensive that would undoubtedly have been suicidal; but the threat of invasion was still there.

"They will not stop at Syria and Palestine," Pharaoh went on, as if reading Meret's thoughts. "Why should they? Why would they forego the wealth and glory of the Kingdom of Two Lands? We shall resist them, certainly. At the first transgression on their part, Egypt will fight. But there is no way we can turn them back. We must seek honorable terms if we wish to prevent our people from being needlessly slaughtered. That is what happened in Palestine and the Phoenician cities." He took a deep breath and spoke in a resigned tone. "In time, Egypt can absorb the Persians— and make Egyptians of them."

Meret, her heart now heavy, asked, "Where will you go, Father?"

"I shall be at the head of my army for as long as the army fights. After that . . . we shall have to wait and see."

"Then I shall be with you, wherever you may go. I'll help you however I can, and together we will find a way to help our country."

Even as she said those idealistic words, Meret felt pangs of anxiety. They were living day by day, as though walking on the edge of a high wall, or like peasants who awaited one of the disastrously high floods that the great Nile brought from time to time. Every luxury and comfort, everything familiar could be swept away overnight. Or maybe not. Who could tell?

Another thought came to Meret's mind. Yes, she was determined to help her father and all Egypt—but how wonderful it had been to help just one person in need! Could she somehow find a way to make a difference in people's health and happiness? Maybe the gods would point out her path . . . if she made herself ready.

Meret looked up at the angle of the sun. It was close to the time when she planned to meet Hector in another garden. They would have much to talk about. Of course, a maidservant would accompany them. . . . Again she thought wistfully of the freedom of the desert.

Hector was living on his nerves these days, knowing that his father's army would soon be called into action and suffer heavy losses. He would probably talk about how galling he found it to be kept in safety, and yet Meret knew he could not stomach slaughter. She would use all her patience and tact to keep up his spirits, no matter how quivery her own. Maybe that was the sort of thing Aset had meant on that emotional morning a lifetime ago.

Then Meret recalled how Hector had fought for her on the docks of Saïs until he was battered and bloody. She felt a little tremor of happiness and thought, It does a woman good to be fought for, at least once in her life. But what next? There, too, Meret felt on the brink of the unknown, for she had no idea how Hector would fit into her life. She only knew that she wanted him there.

Pharaoh, seated quietly on a bench, appeared lost in thought. Meret gave his hand a squeeze, bent over to kiss his cheek, and left the garden.

CHAPTER 29

In the council chamber, after the shouting had died down and most of the military officers had rushed out, and Princess Meret and Hector were well reunited with their anxious fathers, someone noticed Bata again. He was taken down to the kitchen, shown a small room where he could scrub himself clean, given fresh clothes and a hearty meal with meat in it, and offered a comfortable pallet for the night. The next morning, feeling there was nothing more for him to do at the palace, he left quietly.

He went back to his old neighborhood and found work at Ipu's tavern, the spot where he and Hector had drunk beer and made glorious plans together. The tavern—where he spent his time sweeping, running errands, chopping vegetables, and mopping up spills—was not so noble a place to work as the stone carvers' workshop. But Bata did not want to go back to his old master's domain. Even if the men were to accept him, which he strongly doubted, he would have been constantly reminded of the loss of Smendes.

He yearned for something, but his heart, feeling somehow spongy and weakened, did not quite understand what it was. What could he seek, what could he do? He had no talent for making beautiful things, and the thought of learning some new, more practical occupation, such as ropemaking, held no appeal for him. He had no taste whatsoever for fighting, or for adventuring into foreign parts. He knew nothing about how to make plants and animals grow. All he knew was that, through thick and thin, he had successfully cared for the goddess and brought her statue to the place where she belonged.

Yet he wanted more. And it seemed strange to him that he should feel so intensely that he wanted more, having been resigned all his life to very little.

Meanwhile, all of Saïs rejoiced over the safe return of Princess Meret. As Bata trotted around in the tavern and the marketplace, he heard many stories of her adventures and miraculous rescue. If it wasn't the Persians who'd carried her off, people said, then it was brigands or maybe demons. In any case, various deities had led the Egyptian army to the castle where she was held captive. Then she'd been brought back in great pomp and luxury by the highest government officials in the land—just in time to keep Egypt from launching a war that everyone agreed would not have been a good idea at all. Bata listened, nodded, and said nothing.

But one item of news he did welcome. The golden fleet had been rescued and was now making its way back to Saïs. The city would hold a grand festival when the boats arrived, with free beer and honey cakes, music and dancing monkeys.

The rejoicing, however, was short-lived. Before the moon had passed through its phases once more, the Persians attacked. The Egyptian and Greek armies met them in a few encounters in the desert east of the delta. But the army that had rolled over Asia quickly proved once more that it was the power of the day. Pharaoh's men fought until further resistance was clearly useless. Then, rather than subject his country to ruin, Pharaoh yielded and agreed to go into exile.

When Bata heard this, he thought his heart would break. He would have no chance ever to see again his former companion Hector and the beautiful princess Meret, not even just a glimpse on a crowded street. As for his beloved goddess, he had no idea where she had been taken. Presumably to a beautiful shrine in the palace. But without knowing for sure, he could only long hopelessly for the privilege of seeing her once more.

A few days passed, days of frantic hysteria in the city, as both the court and the mercenary Greek army prepared to depart. Then one morning Bata looked up from the kitchen floor where he was squatting to sort lentils, and saw a Greek with polished sword and spotless military tunic standing before him.

"So this is where you've been hiding! Bata, I've looked high and low for you—and it hasn't been easy. Everything's in a hellish mess, and everybody's half crazy these days. Why did you disappear?"

Of course Hector gave him no chance for an explanation and, as Bata got to his feet, went right on talking. "You're wanted at the palace. Meret says she must see you before we leave. Yes, come along, just like that—there's no time for fussing around." He pulled Bata toward the entrance. The tavern keeper made no move to stop them, since these days it was better simply to bend with whatever wind blew.

But once in the street, Hector drew Bata around to face him and gripped Bata's arms with both hands. The tension in his face gave way to a delighted smile.

"Let me look at you, Bata," he said warmly. "Oh, by the gods, I've missed your homely face—that face that never concealed anything false. I've missed your calm and steadiness, your courage and your plain good sense—and even your irrational faith. Oh, Bata, how I've missed *you!*"

As Bata heard this, he felt his heart rising higher and higher, until he feared it might pop out of his mouth. Now he knew one reason why his heart had felt riddled. Hector the impulsive and moody, joyful and rash, brave and true — Hector, who in some unaccountable way seemed to need Bata . . . his absence had left a deep ravine in Bata's life. Bata stammered for words, but none came. All he could do was grin happily and for a moment hold that clean, well-shaped hand in his own grubby, calloused, strong one. Then the two set off at a fast trot through the littered streets.

In the palace, sights of confusion and splendor flashed past Bata's eyes. Hector led him through halls jammed with packed goods and furniture to be taken away. Finally they reached a garden, untended and overgrown but fragrant. There the princess Meret greeted Bata, smiling and more beautiful than he could ever have imagined. Although her face was now properly painted, she wore no wig. Her dark curls danced freely in the breeze.

Then Hector, with a laugh, slid an arm around Meret's waist. "You're seeing right here the only good thing that's happened lately, Bata," he said. "Pharaoh and his court are leaving with the Greek army for the islands, which means that Meret and I will be together — "

She eased away from him a bit but did not lose her smile or the mischievous glint in her eye. "Yes, we'll be together . . . when I'm not too busy learning to read the profound writings in Greek that I've heard so much about."

You were right as usual, O Goddess, thought Bata.

Before Hector could retort, the princess lifted her chin and took on a more serious air. "Come, Bata, we have little time, and there is someone else who wants to speak to you."

Wondering, he followed her obediently to another part of the garden, where golden fish still played in a large pool. There, seated on an ornately carved stone bench, sat Egypt's king, a papyrus document in his hand and several others at his side.

Overwhelmed, Bata could barely glance at the king before dropping to his knees. He threw himself forward, touching his forehead to the pebbled walkway.

"Lift yourself, Bata," he heard Pharaoh say. With a gentle prod from Hector's foot, Bata straightened up, remaining on his knees. He raised his eyes and at last beheld the face of the god-king. It was a kind and intelligent face, the face of a good man.

"Pharaoh knows what you have done, Bata," said Ankh-haf. "He knows of your faithful efforts to carry out the wishes of your master Smendes. He knows of your courage and strength in bringing the princess Meret back to her home. And he is grateful. He wishes to reward you, with whatever remains in his power to bestow. What is your heart's wish, Bata?"

The beautiful words rang in Bata's head. Suddenly, as if a golden bell had announced it to him, he knew what his heart longed for. Gazing directly up at Pharaoh, he spoke.

"O most blessed and mighty Pharaoh, what the lowly Bata wishes for is to spend all his days serving the goddess Taweret—because the gracious Princess Meret told the lowly Bata to be guardian of the goddess, even though we were in the desert then and she probably meant just until we got back to Saïs. But that is what the lowly Bata's heart desires above all things, even just to sweep out the beautiful Taweret's temple every morning, O most blessed and mighty Pharaoh, may thou live forever."

In the silence that followed, Bata lowered his gaze, suddenly stunned at what he had done. How could he possibly dream of serving the goddess, whose statue had been made expressly to protect the princess? But he had spoken truly, just as his heart wanted him to.

Then Princess Meret said, "I think that's the perfect reward. Whatever the future may hold for us, wherever fortune may take us, the goddess belongs in Egypt. Her statue must remain here, and it will require the most devoted care—such as Bata alone can give."

At last Pharaoh responded. "So, Bata, you wish to be a priest to the goddess Taweret? Then that is what you shall be. You shall live at her temple, perform the duties required for her care, acquire priestly learning, and enjoy all the privileges of your office."

Bata sat back on his heels, speechless with amazement and happiness. Coming to his senses, but still on his knees, he backed respectfully away from Pharaoh until he felt Hector nudge him to stand up. As Bata looked at his old companions for what he knew was the last time, Hector again took him by the hand.

"I wish you happiness with your goddess, Bata," he said, "for all your life."

"Long life and happiness to you both," said Bata. And although he wished he could utter a finer speech, his full heart told him that this would do.

Bata left the tavern and went to the temple. It was a small, exquisite temple on the outskirts of the city, beautifully embellished. It was, to be sure, a shared temple. Taweret dwelt in one half, and the cat goddess Bastet in the other. Taweret told Bata that she found Bastet quite an amiable companion, although a bit flighty in her interests. The squad of priests who maintained the temple were pious and generous men. If they felt envy at Pharaoh's appointment of an ignorant young nobody to their ranks, Bata was never made aware of it.

Bata often remembered the many days and nights when he and the goddess had lived in squalor, distress, and the smell of rotting onions, and he had wondered whether he would ever be able to take proper care of her. Now his dream had come true. Every day he awoke her, bathed and dressed her, fed her succulent meals. Then he guided to her lionlike feet the unending stream of humble people who came to seek her blessing . . . for Taweret was no aloof deity, approachable only by priests. She was always ready to welcome those who loved her.

Usually other priests performed the duties with Bata. Sometimes, though, he had time alone with Taweret. Then, in soft voices, they talked about their past adventures and their present world.

"The Sacred City is in a sorry state," Taweret told him. "I hear it from all of my sisters and brothers. The Persians have no interest in permitting that nest of intrigue to fester against them, and they are taking charge with a heavy hand." She chuckled. "I imagine in due time they will let things fall back into place. Egypt's new masters generally do, history shows us."

"We shall see," said Bata. "But, O Goddess, what about the Divine Wife, who was so cruel to Princess Meret?"

"Ah, the Divine Wife. Yes, indeed. She has been stripped of all her possessions, I hear, and is imprisoned for the rest of her life in one small wing of her dark palace, alone with one attendant. The two women bicker ceaselessly. Meanwhile, the great Amun seems to be managing quite happily without a wife."

"Too good for her, the old ape," muttered Bata. "Forgive me, O Goddess."

"You are forgiven," said Taweret.

She was so sensible, Bata thought, as he gazed with love at her long snout with the tip of tongue protruding, her swollen belly, her cowlike ears, her gentle round eyes. And so good. From time to time she had a tendency to brood, as she contemplated the elegance of her sister Bastet, so hand-some and slim, close by. But she always got over it quickly, and Bata admired her all the more for it.

Bata also thought frequently of the days ahead when he would have a young wife. She would provide him with a cheerful, comfortable home, while he would give her love, plenty to eat, and few arguments. And before long, with Taweret's blessing, they would have fine healthy sons and daughters.

But there was one question that still smoldered in Bata's heart, which he had never quite had the courage to ask the goddess. And then, one day, he did.

"O Goddess, do you . . . do you remember my mother?"

Taweret smiled, a smile of such serene beauty that for a moment Bata thought it might be her only answer. "Yes, Bata," she then said. "Your mother was a good woman. She had nothing in life, only you. And she could give you nothing, not even a father . . . nothing but life itself. But when she passed over to the Western Fields, she knew that you would make the most of that life. I assured her of that. Why do you think I kept my eye on you—and found my way to the shop of the master Smendes?"

That was all the goddess ever told Bata, and it was enough.

So Bata went about his duties with joy, confident that whatever new rulers might roll over his country, the old ways—the true ways—would go on and on. His people would believe what it did them good to believe . . . what guided their lives along straight paths. It was Bata's privilege to help preserve the good, and he could not have asked for a happier place in the whole uncertain universe.

AUTHOR'S NOTE

When my sister and I were growing up near Boston, our parents often took us to the famous Museum of Fine Arts. Naturally, the Egyptian rooms — especially the mummies — were always our first stop. Oh, the fascinating sight of those withered toes! Later my interest in ancient Egypt took a literary turn, and in fourth grade I started to write my first novel. Although it never got beyond the third page, I do remember that the hero was not a prince or noble, but an ordinary boy, like Bata.

Sometimes a good book that we read in childhood points us to a lifelong interest or even a career. That was true for me, reading books about ancient Egypt. A few years ago, for an article, I read just about every novel set in ancient Egypt for young people published in the last seventy years or so. These books helped me think of the ancient Egyptians as real, flesh-and-blood people, not the stereotypes of Hollywood movies and TV spectaculars. I've also gotten to know modern Egyptians, having lived in Cairo on many occasions. One special year was 1991, when my husband was the director of the American Research Center in Egypt, which gave me the chance to visit several archaeological digs and study Egyptology.

When researching my book *The Ancient Egyptians,* I learned about the intriguing Twenty-sixth Dynasty. What dramatic possibilities it offered for a story!

The Twenty-sixth Dynasty, also called the Saite Dynasty because its kings lived in the delta town of Saïs, started around 664 B.C. For several centuries prior to this, Egypt had been in a state of decline—fragmented, fought over, ruled by foreigners, invaded, and generally going downhill. King Psamtik I determined to make Egypt a force to be reckoned with once more. First he had to unite all of Egypt, north and south, under his rule. With a strong central government and a beefed-up army, he and his successors then went campaigning again in western Asia.

It wasn't just military prowess, however, that the Saite pharaohs sought. Culturally they wanted to emulate the Age of Pyramids, the Old Kingdom, which had produced some of the finest sculpture, painting, and architecture of ancient Egypt's 3,000-year history. For a few decades, therefore, craftsmen created artwork far superior to anything seen for hundreds of years before—or after.

But Egypt was not safe from the constant rise and fall of superpowers in western Asia (Mesopotamia, Syria, and Palestine). Another army, from Persia, was soon to conquer those lands; and Egypt, too, had to yield. The Persian conquest of Egypt brought an end to the Twenty-sixth Dynasty in 525 B.C.

There was a curious paradox about the Saite pharaohs' rule. While deliberately trying to imitate the Egypt of a much earlier "isolationist" era, they welcomed large numbers of foreigners. Some were traders, but primarily the foreigners were Greek mercenary troops. The Greeks did much of the pharaohs' fighting for them. But they were not popular with the people. Foreign armies rarely are.

Another highlight of the Twenty-sixth Dynasty was the preeminence of a woman. Called the Divine Wife, she was considered the consort of the god Amun, the supreme god in the sacred city of Thebes (the Greek name for the city we know today as Luxor). The office of Divine Wife had started several centuries earlier as an honorary title or as a sort of high priestess, but without much fuss being made over it. Around the start of the Saite Dynasty, however, it was clear that the position of Divine Wife could be a powerful force politically.

When Psamtik was establishing his control over the southern part of the country, around 660 B.C., he sent his fourteen-year-old daughter Nitiqret up the river to Thebes to be the new Divine Wife. She was escorted by a convoy of lavishly equipped royal boats, with great celebration (described in detail on a large stone still in Karnak Temple in Luxor). The existing Divine Wife in Thebes had no choice but to accept Nitiqret as her successor. It seems to have been a flamboyant and completely successful political maneuver, essential in helping to unite Egypt under the Saite pharaoh's rule.

In due course, the aging Nitiqret was succeeded by another young girl, who also lived a long time. In fact, those two ladies reigned as Divine Wife for a total of 134 years! They commanded untold wealth, not just gold but land and its produce. With the backing of the powerful and enormous priesthood, they could appoint the high administrative officers who ran the southern part of the country. In effect, the Divine Wife could make or break the central government of Egypt. Under Persian rule, not surprisingly, the office of Divine Wife was abolished.

A few more notes about Egypt and ancient Egyptian society may interest the reader. The land of Egypt contains many geographical surprises. One, fortunately little known as yet, is the place described in the story as the "white walls." It is a large mysterious uplift rising abruptly from the desert floor, composed of a soft white rock that crumbles into great drifts of sand as white as snow. Like Meret, I spent an uncomfortable night camping in this truly amazing place; and later, like her, I also had a dip in a hot artesian spring in a small oasis. These sites are actually in the desert west of the Nile, but for my story I had to take a little geographic license and move them to the eastern desert.

In the story there are many references to people's hearts. That's because the ancient Egyptians considered the heart all-important as the seat of a person's individual character. It was, they believed, not only the source of emotion, conscience, and feeling (much as we regard it in a figurative sense), but the organ for *thinking* as well. They didn't know what the brain was for; in the process of mummification, therefore, the heart was carefully preserved and the brain was discarded.

Readers may be surprised that Bata and Hector drank so much beer. There was nothing wrong with that, for all Egyptians drank beer. Beer brewing had been going on in ancient Egypt since the fourth millennium, long before the pharaohs. Since it was usually made from barley bread, there was probably some nutritive value to it, and mothers sent their little boys off to school with a good lunch of bread and beer. Beer was very much a part of life, for every class, and people enjoyed it for the same reasons they do today.

The names of the people in my story were chosen with a view to easy readability—as Egyptian names go. They are typical of names that appear throughout ancient Egypt's long history, although not particularly pertinent to the period of the story.

Now, for the Ugly Goddess herself. Why, from all the handsome and interesting deities worshiped in ancient Egypt, did I choose the strangest-looking? In the first place, Taweret was a benevolent, protective deity, appropriate for accompanying a young princess to a place of possible danger. But that wasn't my main reason.

In 1997 while visiting the famed Egyptian Museum in Cairo, I noticed an object displayed near the entrance as the "treasure of the month." It was a statue, about two feet high, of Taweret. Made in the Twenty-sixth Dynasty of an unusually hard stone, it was designed and carved with extraordinary skill and was in perfect condition. It immediately set me to thinking. The nature of beauty, the ways we look at things, the way an artist may follow age-old "rules" yet be driven by individual talent and reverence . . . these ideas, stimulated by this weird-looking statue, launched my new novel.

Two years later, having already written the novel, I was in Egypt again and naturally visited the museum. The statue of Taweret had been moved back to its regular gallery. This time I noticed on its case an explanatory card that I had not seen earlier. This very statue, I discovered, had been made expressly to accompany the Princess Nitiqret on her triumphal journey to Thebes to be the next Divine Wife. Unknowingly, I had repeated history in my story. While the pharaoh Ankh-haf and the princess Meret of my novel are fictitious characters, *The Ugly Goddess* reflects actual history to an extent that surprised even the author!

One other incident struck me on that visit. Several Egyptian art students, young men and women, were sitting on the floor around the statue in its case. While most of them were chatting and flirting, one girl was intent on her drawing. I asked her why she had chosen this particular statue to draw, when there were so many others more appealing in appearance. She looked up at me in surprise and answered simply: "It's beautiful."